W9-AEE-275

Getting Rid of Marjorie

**Other books by Betty Ren Wright
from Apple Paperbacks**

Ghosts Beneath Our Feet
The Dollhouse Murders
The Secret Window

Coming soon
Christina's Ghost

Getting Rid of Marjorie

by
Betty Ren Wright

AN
APPLE®
PAPERBACK

SCHOLASTIC INC.
New York Toronto London Auckland Sydney Tokyo

No part of this publication may be reproduced in whole or in part, or stored in a retrieval system, or transmitted in any form or by any means, electronic, mechanical, photocopying, recording, or otherwise, without written permission of the publisher. For information regarding permission write to Holiday House, Inc., 18 East 53rd Street, New York, NY 10022.

ISBN 0-590-40604-3

Copyright © 1981 by Betty Ren Wright. All rights reserved. Published by Scholastic Inc., 730 Broadway, New York, NY 10003, by arrangement with Holiday House, Inc.

12 11 10 9 8 7 6 5 4 3   7 8 9/8 0 1/9

Printed in the U.S.A.   11

For my husband and my mother
with deepest love,
and for Larry and Eleanor Sternig,
who have made so many
pleasant dreams come true

Getting Rid of Marjorie

Contents

Getting Rid of Marjorie

1 · Terrible News

Emily leaped off the bus and stumbled, almost falling on her knees in her haste to put the ride behind her. Today's trip home from school, the last of the year, had been worse than usual. Jason Timmons had had his father's sterling silver flask hidden in his lunch bag. He had passed it from one person to another, holding his English book around it in an elaborate cover-up so Tog, the bus driver, wouldn't see it. Emily had refused to drink, not just because she hated the taste of whiskey and the raw burning in her throat but because she couldn't put her lips on the mouth of the flask after the other fifth-graders had had their turn. She just couldn't.

"Baby," Jason taunted, pushing the flask at her. "Mama's fat little baby is afraid."

Emily had shoved his hand away. "I'm not," she said furiously. "I'm not afraid of anything. I just—"

"She's a teetotaler," Jean Ellen Cofrin said. Her eyes gleamed crazily; she'd already had two or three sips from the flask. "Just like her dear old granddaddy. My father says her granddaddy is so pure he never drinks anything stronger than melted snow." She laughed, then screamed as Emily leaped at her. Together they rolled from the seat into the narrow, dirty aisle, with everyone shouting and cheering. The next thing Emily knew, the bus had stopped, and Tog's big hands were pulling the fighters apart. He thrust Jean Ellen back into her seat and dragged Emily up front with him.

"Now sit there," he said, dropping her, not ungently, into the empty seat behind him where no one ever sat. "Act like a lady, for pete's sake, or you can walk the rest of the way home."

Emily started to talk back but thought better of it. She was secretly glad to be away from her classmates in the back of the bus, and besides, Tog was capable of carrying out his threat and making her walk.

If only Sally had been there, she thought. If only she didn't take the late bus on Fridays. Sally would have refused to drink, too, but no one ever tried to make *her* do what she didn't want to do. When Sally said No, or Yes, it made all the other girls wish they had said the same thing.

"You're a mess," Tog said, as Emily stood up at her stop. "Better comb your hair before you get home, or your folks will be calling the principal's office to find out what goes on."

You're just worried about your job, Emily told him silently, but when she was free at last, and the bus was out of sight, she raked her fingers through her long dark hair and wiped her face with a crumpled Kleenex. She certainly didn't want her mother asking questions.

Chicory Road was a fragrant contrast to the hot, loud, smelly bus. The grass had turned brilliant along the shoulders, and a delicate mosaic of purple and white appeared like needlepoint stitches on the background of green. At one side of the road were lawns stretching in long, shallow slopes to the ranch houses beyond them, and on the other side was a field, newly plowed and seeded. Beyond everything—houses, lawns, field—were the woods, freshly leafed and inviting.

Emily waited for the good feelings that were part of this homecoming every afternoon. From her toes and fingers a delicious aliveness bubbled right to her brain, and she felt dizzy—no, giddy was the right word. Giddy with the pleasure of being here again, and the particular pleasure of being here at the beginning of vacation. The whole summer lay ahead of her, and tomorrow was a very special day.

First the cookies, she thought, starting to walk faster. The cookie jar had to be full of gingersnaps when her grandfather returned from his California trip tomorrow. Emily gave a little skip, thinking that soon he would be there, with nothing to do but listen. That was one of the best things about him —the way he listened. She could tell him anything—the way the other kids in her class seemed suddenly older than she was, the painful things like what had happened today on the bus. He didn't tattle and he didn't preach. He just listened, and his silence made her feel that he was sorry but not worried. Things would get better, and meanwhile there were walks in the woods and books to read and cookies to share. Good things, right now.

After I finish the cookies, I'll pick some tulips for the vase on his dining-room table, Emily thought. *And I'll make sure there's some popcorn in the cupboard.* Her feet began to fly. Down the road she ran, toward her house and her grandfather's beyond it, with the dust rising in little puffs behind her.

At first when Emily opened her front door she thought no one was home, but then she heard her mother's voice from the kitchen and realized she was talking on the phone. The house smelled of furniture polish and something sweet like cherries. Emily headed toward the kitchen to see what the sweetness was, then slowed as her mother spoke again.

". . . doesn't know yet," her mother was saying. "I told Paul he was more than welcome to the job of telling her. You never know with Emily, but I have a feeling she isn't going to take it well. She's so—" She stopped as Emily came into the kitchen.

"Hi! Don't you dare touch that pie, dear heart," her mother said with forced gaiety, obviously for the benefit of the person on the line, since the pie was on the windowsill, well out of reach. Emily glared at her and sat down at the table, waiting with exaggerated patience for the call to end.

"Tell me what?" she demanded the second her mother hung up. "Take what well?"

Her mother stood up and moved the pie to the counter. "For heaven's sake, why don't you say hello like other people?" she said nervously. "There's no need to snap and snarl at your poor old mother."

"Tell me what?" Emily repeated. It could be something small but unpleasant, like a dentist's appointment, or it could be something simply awful that would destroy the whole beautiful summer. She had to know at once.

"We'll talk about it when your father gets home," her mother said.

Emily felt desperate. Often her mother didn't even recognize the difference between big catastrophes and small ones.

"Now," she pleaded. "Tell me right *now.*"

"Don't whine, Emily. Whining is for babies, and you're a big girl now."

Her mother's tone made arguing hopeless. Emily jumped to her feet and thumped her school books on the table.

"I'm going over to Grandpa's house," she said. "There're some things I want to do before he gets home."

"Wait!" The response was so sharp that Emily stopped short.

"It's something about Grandpa," she said. "He's not sick, is he? He's not—" Emily couldn't say the word. It was a word that had nothing to do with her grandfather and never would.

"No, he's fine." Her mother looked at her worriedly. "It's just a decision he's made— I really want this to wait till your father gets home, Emily."

"A decision? He isn't moving away? He isn't!" She managed to say the words, though the thought of his moving out of the big house down the road was almost as painful as the thought of his dying. Emily had heard her parents discuss the possibility more than once in the two years since her grandmother's death. The house was too large for one person, they said, and too full of memories. As if memories could hurt you. When Emily had asked her grandfather if he wanted to move, he had always laughed and told her to stop worrying. "This is home," he said. He wouldn't have lied to her about something so important, and she couldn't believe he would change his mind without talking to her first.

"No," her mother said. "He isn't moving away."

"Then *what?*"

Her mother turned and began taking plates and glasses out of the cupboard. "He's married," she said. "Your grandfather was married last week in California."

Emily sat down again. "I don't believe you," she said rudely.

"It's true, dear. He called the night before last to tell us. His new wife is someone he worked with for many years in Milwaukee. She was transferred to Los Angeles about ten years ago, and when Grandpa went out there, he looked her up right away. It turned into a—a little romance, and they decided to get married."

"A little romance!" Emily bellowed. She wanted to throw up. "You make it sound like some stupid play on television! Grandpa doesn't need a wife—he had one! He had Grandma Ellen." She felt tears on her cheeks, and her voice shook. "Why would he marry somebody else?"

Her mother turned around and faced her. "I suppose he was lonely," she said. "He may seem like an old man to you, but he really isn't. He wants to get out and do things, and he wants someone with him. He needs companionship."

Emily glared. "He has companionship!" she roared. "He has a nice dog and a cat. He has *me!* And I never thought he was old. Never! You don't know how I feel about anything!"

Emily pushed back her chair and ran out of the kitchen, ignoring her mother's loud sigh. "I'll never speak to him again," she shouted from the foot of the stairs, then ran upstairs to her bedroom.

An hour later her mother knocked on the door and opened it.

"I'd like you to go over to Christophers' and get Tony," she said, her voice carefully neutral. "It's getting late, and I don't like him to come home through the woods alone."

"Okay." Emily kept her face turned to the wall until the door closed again. Actually, she was glad to go to Christophers'. She had cried herself out and was ready to tell Sally what had happened. Sally would understand how she felt; she always did.

Slowly Emily got up from the rumpled bed and went to the mirror over her bureau. Her round face was flushed and terrible looking—even more terrible than usual. She scowled and watched the heavy black brows almost meet above her nose. *Like a witch,* she thought. *If I was really a witch, I'd put a spell on you-know-who the minute she gets here.*

In the hour since she'd heard the news, Emily had come to some decisions. First, it would be impossible not to talk to her grandfather in the future. They wouldn't be special friends any more, but she couldn't bear not to talk to him at all. You-know-who was another matter entirely. Emily would not speak to the new wife or even look at her. She would pretend she was invisible. And if her grandfather bothered to ask why, she would say there was nothing wrong at all. Let him wonder. Let him worry. She brushed her hair furiously.

Let him enjoy his stupid old companionship!

2 · Nobody Cares

"I bet she married your grandfather for his money," Sally said. They had separated their five-year-old brothers with some difficulty, and now they were walking back toward Emily's house with Tony scuffing along behind them. "He's pretty rich, isn't he?"

Emily was surprised. "I don't think so," she said. "He's just average." She wished Sally hadn't suggested such a thing. As much as she resented the woman who had married her grandfather, she couldn't imagine her marrying him for a reason like that.

"Well, he certainly has the nicest house around here," Sally said. "And the biggest lawn. Maybe he showed her a picture of his house and she thought, 'That's just where I'd like to live.' And so she married him. Why else would old people get married?"

Emily was silent. She didn't like to contradict her friend, who was almost always right, but there was something insulting about Sally's analysis, as there had been in her mother's comments earlier. "A little romance." A husband who was desirable only because he was rich. The words didn't fit her grandfather. Everything about him was vigorous, warm, straightforward. When he was happy, his eyes shone, and even though he said little, his pleasure was obvious. When he was hurt or disappointed in you, his silence became painful, and he seemed to retreat without moving an inch. You knew where you stood with him—it was one of the best things about him—and he always understood your feelings. If anyone had thought, "I like this man because he's rich," he'd have known it and walked away. Emily was sure of it.

"Anyway," Sally went on briskly, "you don't have to be nice to her. She has no right to take your grandmother's place and move into her house when she's dead and can't defend herself."

"Right." Emily was relieved that the conversation had shifted into an area of complete agreement. "I hate her already. I'm never going to speak to her, but if I did I'd tell her I had a perfectly fine grandmother who died and nobody could ever take her place."

"Where are your other grandparents?" Sally asked. "Your Mom's mother and dad?"

"They live in Hawaii," Emily said. "I might as well not have them at all. Except for Christmas and birthdays."

Sally glanced over her shoulder. "I bet Tony hardly remembers your real grandmother," she said. "How old was he when she died?"

Emily figured. "Three. And the babies weren't even born. They never knew Grandma Ellen."

"Then it'll be up to you to tell them about her when they

get older," Sally said. "Otherwise they'll think this new person is just great. Especially if she's pretty and makes a fuss over them."

Tony pushed between them. "What new person?" he demanded. "What are you talking about?"

The girls looked at each other. "Ask Daddy tonight," Emily said after a moment. "He'll tell you."

"You said 'hate,'" Tony went on, pleased to find himself part of the conversation. "The Bible says you shouldn't hate anyone. I'm going to tell Daddy."

"The Bible also says thou shalt not be a fink," Emily retorted. "So just forget this whole conversation—or else!"

Luckily they had reached their backyard, and Tony was distracted by the sight of his tricycle.

Emily's mother appeared at the kitchen window carrying the twins.

"Please go over to your grandfather's and feed Barney and Pumpkin," she called. "Your father will be home soon, and we'll eat in about forty-five minutes. I'm going to feed the babies now."

Emily wanted to protest, but if she argued it would mean that her grandfather's pets would have to wait for their dinner.

"Go with me," she begged Sally. "I don't want to go there alone."

The feeling of not belonging grew as Emily walked down the gravel road with Sally. In the space of a couple of hours this end of the road, where the woods crowded in on either side, had become alien territory, the province of strangers. It was the time of day Emily usually enjoyed most, when the shadows deepened and the birds sounded muted and sleepy. She had never been afraid of the darkened woods because, as long as she could remember, the lights in her grandparents' house had glowed beyond the trees, like a warm invitation. But tonight, of course, there were no lights, and, Emily reflected bleakly, they would not shine again for her.

"I want to tell you something," Sally said. "I know you're upset, but I have to tell you. I'm going to do something really special this summer."

"You're going away?" The words were out, a wail of anguish, before Emily could stop them. "I won't have any-body—"

Sally squeezed her arm. "I'm not going away," she said. "I'm going to write a book!"

"A book?"

"And draw the pictures for it, too. I made up this story for Jimmy last winter, and my uncle says it's really good. He ought to know because he works in a bookstore and he knows some editors. I'm going to write the story, and then I'm going to draw pictures to go with it, and I'm going to ask my uncle to show it to his editor friends. Maybe they'll print it!"

Stunned, Emily forgot for a moment her own unhappiness. "Oh, Sal, that's terrific! A real book! You'll be famous."

Sally tried to look doubtful without succeeding. "Maybe I will be. I haven't told my uncle what I'm going to do because I want to surprise him. But I wanted you to know since it'll take a lot of my time this summer."

"He'll love it," Emily said. "And his editor friends will love it, too. You're the best artist in our class. And the best writer. You'll probably go to New York and have autograph parties and be on talk shows and everything." She babbled on, trying hard to quell the sputtering envy inside her. *She's my best friend, and I'm really glad she's going to be famous.* "I'm really glad for you, Sal."

In spite of herself, the words had a hollow ring. Sally looked at her curiously. "What are *you* going to do this summer?"

It was a question Emily hadn't even asked herself before today. "I don't know. Nothing, I guess. Just nothing, except help with the babies. I'm not good at anything, and you'll be busy, and my grandfather—"

The house loomed ahead of them, a pale and lovely ghost reminding her of good times gone by. From his doghouse in back, Barney barked a welcome, and the orange cat Pumpkin glided toward them with shining eyes.

This is probably the last time I'll come here, Emily thought, and she began to cry.

Sally put an arm around her. "Please don't," she said. "There's lots of fun things you can do this summer. We'll do them together. I'm not going to work on my book all the time." She paused. "Are you thinking about your grandfather? Is that it? Because if it is, I'm sure you'll feel better tomorrow. After all, he's still your grandfather. Nothing's really changed."

Emily gave her a look. This time Sally did *not* understand. "I don't want to talk about it," Emily said. "I'm okay." But she wasn't. Sally had hair like yellow silk and two perfectly healthy, conveniently located sets of grandparents. Her mother wasn't busy all the time taking care of two small babies. Sally could write and draw, and when she said something, people listened. She was going to be famous. What did she know about trouble?

Pumpkin wrapped himself around Emily's ankles, and she bent to pick him up. "I wish—" she said softly. "I just wish—"

"—that you could write a book, too?" Sally offered.

"—that it was this morning," Emily said. "That this day hadn't happened at all."

Emily's father took twice as long as usual to drink his before-dinner highball. Usually when he dawdled, her mother fretted about keeping the dinner warm, but tonight she gave Tony his meal in the kitchen and didn't say a word.

"I'm hungry," Emily said, when it became clear that no one else was going to complain. "I want to eat."

Her father put down his newspaper and looked at her. "Your mother says she told you about Grandpa's marriage," he said. "She tells me you weren't exactly thrilled."

Emily twisted in her chair. Her father always sounded sarcastic, even when he didn't mean to be. She wondered if he meant to be now.

"Well, how *do* you feel about it?" he asked.

"I don't care."

Her father raised his eyebrows and Emily sighed, noting that his glass was still almost half full. More questions, she thought. It was what happened if your father was an attorney. Sally's father was an accountant, and he hardly ever asked her anything.

"Your mother seemed to think you were upset. Angry. Hurt. Is that how you feel?"

Emily curled her feet under her and wrapped her arms around her stomach. "I just think it's stupid, that's all. He doesn't need a wife. He had Grandma Ellen for years and years, and now he's forgotten all about her. I should think you'd feel bad, too." She knew her anger was getting out of control, but she couldn't stop. "I should think you wouldn't like it one bit, having him pick out a new mother for you when you didn't even ask for one."

Her father's face reddened. "She's hardly a mother-substitute, since she's only about fifteen years older than I am. And, as you so sweetly point out, I really don't want or need another mother. The one I had was more than satisfactory. But your grandfather deserves a life of his own, and he has the right to make his own decisions. Remember that."

"You don't like it either," Emily said. "I can tell."

"Whether I like it or not is hardly the point. I'll agree that the marriage came as a surprise, but it's happened, and when they get here tomorrow we're all going to make Marjorie welcome. Do you understand?"

Marjorie. It was the first time Emily had heard you-know-who's name. Marjorie. She stared at her father and saw that his face was stiff with anger and something else. Was it sadness? For a moment she felt sorry for him. Was he thinking about a stranger handling his mother's dishes, rearranging the furniture, reading her books? Maybe he felt like crying, too. Then Emily reminded herself that he was going to go along with the marriage and was ordering her to accept it. Nobody cared as much as she did.

"Emily, do you hear me?"

"I hear you," Emily said.

Her mother called from the dining room with phony cheerfulness, "Come on, you two. The pork chops are going to turn to leather if we wait much longer."

Her father stood up and motioned Emily to lead the way.

"Let's not forget this little talk," he said. "I think we understand each other."

But we don't, Emily thought. *We never do. Our little talks always end up nowhere.* And she felt like crying all over again at the thought of her grandfather who always understood, even when she found it hard to say what she was thinking, and who was coming home tomorrow with Marjorie, his new companion.

3 · The Homecoming

"But I don't wanna go with you," Tony protested. "I wanna stay here in front of the house and watch for Grandpa."

Emily, hands on hips, glared at him. "This is a very private conversation we're going to have," she growled. "I have to talk to you for just a couple of minutes." When Tony ignored her, she tried bribery. "Half a Milky Way bar, and tomorrow I'll hold you on my bike so you can pretend you're riding. Okay?"

Tony stared down the road a moment or two longer, then gave in. "You'll have to hurry up," he said. "I wanna be here when they come home."

They cut across the yard and into the woods, following the narrow path that led to Christophers' house and the next road west. The sun-dappled ground was dotted with columbine and wild geraniums, and overhead a woodpecker rapped out his familiar code. Ordinarily Emily would have walked slowly, enjoying the fresh loveliness of the day, but this afternoon she thought only of what she wanted to say to her little brother.

A hundred feet along the path there was a tiny clearing where an oak tree had fallen, taking a couple of birches with it. Emily sat down on a log, and Tony crouched a couple of feet away.

"It's about Grandma," she began, suddenly nervous because this was important and she wanted to do it right.

"The old grandma or the new one?" Tony asked.

"That's exactly it. There is only one, Tony. Besides the grandma in Hawaii, I mean. We had a wonderful grandma —Grandma Ellen—who lived down the road. She died, and now we have to remember her and love her."

Tony frowned. "But I *don't* remember her," he said. "Not much, anyway."

Sally had been right. "Well, you must remember something about her," Emily insisted. "Tell me every little thing you can think of."

Silence. Then, "She was sick in bed a lot, and she was very happy when I came to visit her." He smiled. "That's all."

"Think again."

He sighed. "She took us to town with her and bought coffee ice-cream cones, and mine fell on the sidewalk. I think she bought me another one."

"She did, she did," Emily said eagerly. "She was always buying us things and taking us places before she got sick. To Chicago to see the Christmas tree at Fields'. To the circus and to the county fair, remember? And she baked the best chocolate cakes in the whole world, with fudge frosting and banana filling because you liked banana best. Don't you remember that?"

"I think so. She made cookies, too."

"Oh, she did! Hundreds of them. Thousands of them. Sometimes, after she got sick, you and I took our sandwiches over there at noon, and we sat on the patio and ate with her. And there were cookies or cake for dessert, no matter how sick she was. Grandma Ellen was perfect!"

"Yes," Tony said agreeably. "She was."

"And nobody can take her place. Nobody."

Tony began to catch the direction the conversation was taking. "Daddy says we have to be nice to the new gr—to the new person—and make her glad to be here. He says she might be lonesome at first."

"No one is forcing her to come," Emily said. "She didn't have to marry Grandpa and leave all her good friends out in Los Angeles."

Tony stood up and hitched his jeans around his narrow waist. "If she's not going to be the new grandma, then what do I call her?"

Emily pretended to consider the question, although she had an answer ready. "I think Mrs. Parker would be best," she said. "Her first name is Marjorie, but it would sound kind of fresh for a five-year-old child to call her that."

Tony started down the path, apparently feeling he had earned his half-a-Milky Way. "What are *you* going to call her?" he asked over his shoulder. "You're an eleven-year-old child."

Emily stood up. "I'm not going to call her anything," she said. "I'm not going to have anything to do with her." She liked the way that sounded and promptly called up another phrase that had rattled around in her head during the long restless night. "I'm going to keep Grandma Ellen's memory alive," she said. "That's what I care about."

Emily caught up to Tony. "That's what I care about, too," he said. For a brief moment he clutched her hand, then let it go. Emily saw that he was beginning to worry.

Now we'll see, she thought. It was what she had wanted, to make him aware of the terrible thing that had happened in their lives, and she had succeeded. Oddly, she was not as pleased as she had expected to be. There was no reason to feel guilty, she told herself. Five was old enough to think. But when Tony reached for her hand again, she squeezed it and tried to call up something else, something pleasant to talk about on their way back to their house.

It could have been just any Saturday, unless you knew the clues that showed this day was different. First of all, Emily's father was cutting the grass for the second time in ten days and without being coaxed. That was a little miracle. He had fussed around the house all morning, moving from his desk to his workbench and back again, with frequent stops in the kitchen for coffee. When the lawn mower began its noisy belching in the garage, Emily saw her mother nod and heard her quick little sigh of relief.

Her mother's Saturday had been different, too. She had spent an hour or more at Grandpa's house, opening windows, dusting, and sweeping the kitchen floor where Pumpkin had scattered cat food.

"I could use some help over there," her mother had announced at the breakfast table, but she didn't argue when Emily shook her head.

"I'll change the beds here and put the dishes in the dishwasher. And I'll take care of Polly and Jane." Emily's mother smiled at this final offer, and Emily grinned back in spite of her black mood. They both knew that she didn't mind caring for her little sisters, even though she often complained about how much trouble they were.

"Dress them in the pink-checked outfits," her mother said, and Emily's grin slipped away. The pink-checked rompers were the babies' best—another indication that this was supposed to be a special occasion.

Only Tony had enjoyed a typical Saturday, spending the morning and the early part of the afternoon with Jimmy Christopher. When their space vehicles finally landed, so that Jimmy could go to town for new shoes, Tony had come back to earth and the present by degrees, finally remembering that his grandfather was about to return. Now, with Emily's warning clearly in mind, he was back at his post in the front yard, his expression both eager and anxious.

Emily watched him from her bedroom window. Behind her, in the playpen, Polly cooed cheerfully and Jane tried to eat her toes.

I'll see that Tony remembers you, Grandma Ellen, Emily promised. *And when the babies get older, I'll talk to them about you all the time.*

It was a real task she was taking on, and she knew it. Ladies always loved Tony, and he was an easy mark. Emily gritted her teeth, imagining him sitting on Marjorie's lap, grinning up at her with his ragged grin. Oh, she would be charming; Emily didn't doubt that. Otherwise she never could have attracted Grandpa, who already had as full and happy a life as a man could wish for.

Emily imagined that Marjorie would look like Grandma Ellen—tall and big-boned, with graying blond hair brushed into a twist at the back of her neck. She was glad her grandfather and her mother had sorted through all of Grandma Ellen's clothes and given them to charities. At the time it had seemed a harsh thing to do, but if they had remained in the closets, Marjorie would soon be wearing them.

Ghastly, Emily thought and made a mental note to repeat the word to Sally. It was the kind of word writers liked.

"Here they come!"

Emily's stomach lurched as Tony started running down the road. After a moment, the familiar blue Buick came into sight, moving slowing because her grandfather always tried to keep down the dust on the road.

The door opened below, and Emily's mother came out on the front lawn. She was wearing her best pants suit, the blue one, and she walked to the side of the house and said something. The lawn mower stopped. Emily moved back from the window as her mother reappeared with her father a step or two behind. The car door slammed.

"Grandpa!" Tony's voice was shrill, and there was a burst of laughter. He had, no doubt, made one of his flying leaps into Grandpa's arms. Emily heard the low growl of her grandfather's voice, and then there was a polite murmur as everyone talked at once.

Gushing, Emily thought fiercely. Her parents didn't want Grandpa to have a new wife any more than she did, but they put on smiling masks and pretended to be pleased. They didn't dare to be honest. What kind of example was that?

"Emily." Her mother's call sounded falsely sweet. "Your

grandfather's here and waiting to see you. Bring the twins with you."

Emily edged around the playpen and stood in front of the mirror. Her image glared back at her, the thick brows drawn to aching tightness. Her long hair was in a tangle, and her stomach strained against her ragged jeans. She was wearing her oldest T-shirt, the one with a rip in one shoulder. She looked awful. If she had to go down, and she knew she did, Marjorie and Grandpa would see how little she cared about this homecoming. One member of the family, at least, would show her real feelings.

Emily picked up Jane and was not sorry to discover that the baby needed changing. *We'll see how she likes smelly infants,* she thought.

"Emily!" This time it was Grandpa who called. She took a deep breath, picked up Polly in her other arm, and went downstairs.

It would have been better if she had been outside with the others when Grandpa and Marjorie arrived. For as she stood at the screen door, waiting for them to notice her, a bright voice called "Hi!" and they all turned toward the side yard.

"Oh, Bill," burbled the new wife at Grandpa's side, "you said she was smart but you didn't tell me she was beautiful. Look at that hair!"

It was Sally, standing there in the late afternoon sun and glowing like a candle.

"Hi," she said again, her voice just slightly quivery under the weight of their attention. "I'm—I'm just Sally, Mrs. Parker. Emily's friend."

"Oh, dear," said Emily's mother.

"Emily, get out here!" her father roared.

Then her grandfather was striding up the path to the front door. "Here come my three gorgeous granddaughters," he shouted. And that was almost the worst of all. Worse than looking like a tramp when Sally looked like an angel. Worse than having to be civil to Marjorie. Because her grandfather had called her gorgeous, and for the first time in all the long, wonderful years that she had loved him, he sounded like a phony.

4 · The World's Falling Apart

They sat in a circle in the living room, all except Emily, who slouched in the doorway and studied the toes of her sneakers. She knew she was making the others uncomfortable, but she didn't care. She despised them all, including Sally who had followed them inside and now clearly wished she hadn't.

"Drink, anyone?" Emily's father jumped to his feet and looked at Marjorie. Emily wondered what he was thinking. Did he think she was pretty? Probably. She was tiny and slim, with smooth olive skin, and he always said he favored brunettes. She wore pale green pants and a loose green tunic, with a chain of bright-colored wooden beads that reached nearly to her waist. *Cute as a button,* Emily thought savagely. *Men!*

"You mustn't bother, Paul." What a dumb voice she had, scratchy sounding! "Well, do you have some fruit juice?"

"Of course. There's a whole pitcher of juice in the refrigerator." That was Emily's mother sounding thrilled, as if Marjorie's asking for a glass of juice was the cleverest thing she had ever heard of. Her mother had just finished taking the twins upstairs to change them and put them down for their naps. Now she was sitting on the sofa, smiling, smiling, until Emily thought her face would surely crack.

"I'll have the same," Grandpa said. "Let me help, Paul." He jumped up and went out to the kitchen, giving Emily a quick hug as he passed her. She kept her body stiff, almost losing her balance in her determination not to respond. If her grandfather noticed, he didn't show it. She could hear his deep voice in the kitchen, describing the trip back from California, and her father's responses. Tony followed them, edging past Emily with care.

"Well." Emily's mother added another volt or two to her smile and leaned toward Marjorie. "You and Dad Parker really surprised us all."

"I'm sure we must have," Marjorie said. "To tell the truth, we even surprised ourselves. I can hardly believe that a month ago I was going off to work every morning and not making any personal decisions bigger than what to wear that day."

And I'll bet you gave that a lot of thought. Emily sneaked a sideways glance at Sally.

"What kind of work do you—did you—do?"

"Office management. I was manager at the Carver Company in Milwaukee years ago. That's where Bill and I met. After my parents died, I needed a complete change, so I sold everything here and moved to Los Angeles. Carver had a branch office there, and later I found a position I liked even more." Marjorie leaned forward and, after a hasty glance toward the kitchen, hurried on, her voice lower now and scratchier than ever. "I've never lived in the country before. I'm . . . concerned!"

"Concerned?" Emily's mother repeated the word, and her too-bright smile faded to a look of confusion.

"I mean, do you have much trouble out here? Break-ins, vandalism, home invasions—that sort of thing? Bill told me he lived outside the city, but I wasn't prepared for such isolation."

Emily was so astonished that she forgot her determination not to look up. Marjorie's face was taut and not pretty at all. She looked scared to death.

"Oh, you mustn't worry about things like that," Emily's mother said. "Dad Parker—Bill—will tell you, we've never had a burglary or any kind of problem in all the years we've been out here. Chicory Road is a dead end, you know, and we get very little traffic. There's nothing but woods beyond here."

Marjorie shivered. "That's what bothers me," she said. "I suppose it sounds silly to you, but I don't like woods. Not at all! And I don't like being away from people. I'm a city person, I guess."

"But it's much more dangerous in the city than it is here, Mrs. Parker," Sally said. "This is the nicest place in the world to live in. There's room to do things, and your friends aren't far away, even if you can't look out the window and see them. Emily and I are together every day."

Sally was trying to make up, Emily knew. Trying to make up for being beautiful, for being the kind of golden girl a grandfather would be proud to introduce to his new wife. Well, it wasn't Sally's fault that she was perfect. Emily rolled her eyes at her friend to let her know she was forgiven.

"Here we are, ladies. Something to soothe the fevered

brow." Emily looked at her father as he pushed past her with
a tray. Fevered brow! He was certainly uptight. Her grandfather was right behind him, and this time he put his arm
around Emily's shoulders and pulled her into the living room
with him.

"Sit down, Emily," he ordered. "Tell me what you've been
up to the last few weeks. I'm sure I've missed a lot."

"There's nothing to tell," Emily said.

It was the first lie she had ever told him. If he had come
home alone, if things were the way they always had been,
Emily would have had a list of secrets a mile long ready to
share when they were alone. She would have told him about
Jason Timmons calling her a baby because she wouldn't
drink from his father's flask. She would have told him how
silly most of the girls in her class had become—calling up
boys and whispering secrets all the time. She would have told
him that Sally was her only real friend, and maybe that was
just because they happened to live near each other. And that
she felt dull and stupid next to Sally. And that she wanted
to be good at something. Anything! They were all things she
had been saving to tell him.

"Life is full of problems," he might say. "But we do sur-
vive somehow. You're a strong person, Emily." When
he said that, she had always *felt* strong. After all, no one
knew her as well as he did. But she needed to hear him
say it.

And now they couldn't talk. Before, when Emily told him
secrets, it had been like putting them into a vault where no
one else could find them. But now there was cute little Marjorie, his companion, and secrets wouldn't be safe with him any
more.

Her grandfather looked at her, eyebrows raised, and she saw that he finally realized something was wrong. "I'm sure we have lots to talk about," he said. "Marjorie and I are going to be pretty busy getting unpacked tonight, but how about a hike tomorrow morning?"

"I can't," Emily said. "I have plans."

"Emily!" Her mother's voice was raised in warning.

"She'll be glad to go, Dad," her father said. "She needs the exercise. She's turning into a crotchety old lady."

Emily started to protest, but her grandfather interrupted. "It's all right," he said. "We'll do it another time. Right, Emily?"

She nodded without looking at him. He was talking to her as if she were a child, a baby to be soothed!

"Well, I'm sure you two will have plenty of time to get caught up on the news later," Marjorie said brightly. "And you certainly do have hiking space, don't you?"

With Grandpa back in the room, she was trying to sound as if she thought the country was great. He turned to her with a pleased expression.

"I'm going to make a hiker out of you, too, my dear," he said. "Wait till you see these woods with the wildflowers in full bloom."

"I'm sure they're beautiful," Marjorie said. "Of course, I've never been much of a walker."

Grandpa chuckled. "That's because of your shoes." They all looked at her tiny green sandals with their incredibly high heels. *Like needles,* Emily thought with contempt. *She'll break her neck the first time she steps outside the door.*

"We'll get you some good boots," he went on. "And some blue jeans. I bet you don't even own a pair of jeans." He said that as if not owning jeans was something to be proud of.

"We'll see," Marjorie said. "All of this is going to take some getting used to, isn't it?"

"Worried about becoming a country girl?" Emily's father asked. "Well, I guess Los Angeles *is* about a million miles away from Chicory Road. Still, it's been a while since we've seen any Indians in the woods."

"Really, Paul," her mother said. She seemed to be trying to send him some kind of warning, but Emily's father kept smiling at them all as if he had said something witty.

Tony spoke for the first time. "Horse pooh," he said. "You have to be careful."

"What on earth?" their mother snapped.

Marjorie leaned toward him. "What did you say, dear?"

"You can't wear those pretty shoes in the woods," Tony explained. "People ride their horses on those paths, and you might step in—"

"Oh, I see." Marjorie put out her hand and, exactly as Emily had predicted, Tony ran and sat beside her. "I'll be very careful," she promised, and her soft, scratchy voice made it sound as if she and Tony were sharing a secret.

Grandpa laughed, and after that the conversation became the kind of weather-politics-books talk grown-ups liked. It was as if the laughter had pulled a plug, and the electricity that had charged the room had suddenly leaked away. Emily saw that Sally was as bored as she was. After a few minutes the girls excused themselves and went out into the late afternoon sunshine.

"Well, what do you think?" Emily asked, when they were a safe distance from the living-room windows.

Sally looked thoughtful. "I don't think she's so bad," she said, then added cautiously, "do you?"

"I think she's ghastly," Emily said. "She's horrible! I can't understand how my grandfather could marry a silly, scaredy person like that."

"Well, she certainly is different from your real grandma," Sally agreed. "And I don't think she's going to like living here very much."

"That's fine with me," Emily replied. "I hope she hates it. I hope she hates it so much she packs up tomorrow and goes right back to California where she belongs."

"Still, she was trying to make everyone like her," Sally said. "I felt kind of sorry for her."

Emily jammed her fingers into the waistline of her jeans and looked up at the sky. Clouds were gathering over the tree tops in shaggy, gray-white masses.

"You only like her because she said you were beautiful," Emily said. "Big deal."

"I do not!" Sally sounded hurt. "I know I'm not beautiful." She stood there, in front of a forsythia bush, waiting for Emily to say something and looking prettier than ever. When the silence stretched out, Sally started toward the path that led through the woods to her road. "I'm going home."

"See you tomorrow," Emily said, but her friend shook her head without looking back.

"I'm going to start my book tomorrow," she said.

And that was that. Emily stared after her. "Well, if that's the way you want to be, okay," she said, too softly to be heard beyond the forsythia bush. But it was no use pretending she didn't care. She had been rude to Sally, and now she had lost her, too.

The whole darn world's falling apart, she thought. It was all Marjorie's fault.

5 · Emily's Project

Emily sat up with a squeak of fright. Lightning lit her room, followed by a crash of thunder that shook the bed. The rain, blowing through the open window, was crossing the room in a fine spray. Her face was wet.

Emily closed the window and was hopping back across the soaked carpet when the lamp flicked on. Her mother's voice made her jump again.

"What a mess! I'll be right back." Her mother disappeared down the hall and returned with an armful of towels. Together she and Emily knelt and pressed the towels into the carpet, absorbing as much of the water as possible.

"I can't imagine why I didn't hear this coming," her mother grumbled. "I usually get in here and close the west window at the first sound of thunder, but this time I slept right through the warnings."

"Me, too," Emily said. "Guess I was really knocked out."

She didn't tell her mother how glad she was to have been awakened. Her dreams had not been pleasant, and the final one, broken off by the storm, remained uncomfortably clear.

Emily had been walking down the road in the dark, toward her grandfather's house, the lights of her own house getting smaller and dimmer behind her. There were no lights at all up ahead. Suddenly she had the feeling that she was being followed. She stopped, listening for footsteps, but there was no sound. Still, she knew danger was close by. She began to run, reaching at last the curving driveway that led to her grandfather's front door. Gravel crunched under her feet, and now she could hear other steps, drawing close in the dark. The driveway seemed endless, but finally Emily reached the house. Where was the big front door? Sobbing, she ran her hands over the wooden siding, trying to find a doorknob. It wasn't there. Then lightning struck close by, and in the split second before she woke she saw the whole front of the house. There were no doors, and no windows either. Just the smooth white siding, with her grandfather and safety on the other side.

"You'd better get into some dry pajamas," her mother said. "Your knees are wet. I'll put another blanket on the bed."

Emily took pajamas from a bureau drawer and went down the hall to the bathroom to change. She never undressed in front of her mother any more, but this time she had another reason for changing in the bathroom. Its window faced south, and she wanted to see the windows in her grandfather's house. It was silly, of course—a dream was just a *nothing*—but when she saw a sprinkling of yellow lights beyond the trees she sighed with relief.

Emily took a drink of water and returned to her bedroom. Her mother was sitting on the side of the bed, watching the rain beat against the windows. "I feel like tucking you in," she said. "Is that allowed?"

Emily shrugged but climbed quickly under the covers. She lay very still while her mother folded the sheet neatly over the top of the blanket, then bent and kissed her on the forehead. "It's going to be all right, Emily," she said. "You have to give things time." With a final pat, she drifted out of the bedroom, turning off the lamp as she went.

It was amazing how once in a while her mother could zero in on trouble and other times be so unaware of what was going on. Not that she believed those comforting words, of course. Yesterday had been a disaster, and tomorrow would undoubtedly be another, but it was nice to know someone was concerned. Her mother was a good person. Most of the time she was better with babies than she was with eleven-year-olds, but she tried. That was important.

Emily turned over in bed, dismissing the lightning that flashed across her closed lids. "I won't think about Grandpa and I won't think about Sally," she whispered to herself. And surprisingly, she didn't. When she woke again, blue sky sparkled outside her closed windows, and the bedroom was very warm.

Emily's father, who often made Sunday breakfast, was banging around in the kitchen when she went downstairs. Tony was in the backyard drying off his swing and slide with a clutch of paper towels, and Jane and Polly were in their playpen in the living room.

Her father waved at her. "How are you today, Sunshine?"

"Okay." Emily sat down at the table, and he forked three

pancakes onto her plate. She dropped a large pat of butter in the center and slid it around with her knife before pouring on maple syrup.

"Still grumpy?"

"I'm not grumpy." Emily hunched over the pancakes and made a hole in the center to let the syrup pour in.

Her father filled his own plate and sat down opposite her. "Your mother's going to sleep late," he said. "The storm kept her awake. I bet it kept Marjorie awake, too. They don't have many like that in smoggy old L.A."

"Their lights were on," Emily said and then could have bitten her tongue. She didn't want her father to think she was spying—or interested.

He didn't seem to notice. "I think it would be a good idea if you went for that walk with your grandfather this morning," he said. "Whatever else you were going to do can wait."

Emily scowled. "I don't like walking."

"You could have fooled me. I thought you loved it."

"Well, I don't want to today." Emily's father was killing her appetite. She thought about getting up and walking out, but when she looked up, she saw that his expression was serious. "I wish you'd do it, Emily. And I want you to make Marjorie feel welcome. Your mother thinks she may not be happy here, so far out in the country and everything so different from what she's been accustomed to. Your mother thinks she could be quite miserable if we don't all try to help."

How miserable? Miserable enough to go back to Los Angeles? Miserable enough to get a divorce? What was so terrible about that?

You'd *better* care," her father said, proving that, like her mother, he could read her mind once in a while. "If Marjorie decides she can't stand country living, she might convince your grandfather that they ought to move into Milwaukee. Or even back to California. You wouldn't like that, I'm sure."

Emily glared at him. "It wouldn't happen," she said. "Not in a hundred million years. Grandpa loves the country and he loves his house. He wouldn't leave here, ever. He told me so lots of times."

"He didn't have anyone else to think about then." Her father refilled his coffee cup and stared into it as if he were reading the future. "Just keep that possibility in mind," he said. "And behave yourself."

He picked up the sports section of the Sunday paper, and Emily saw that the conversation was over. For a moment her father had frightened her, but now she reminded herself of how her grandfather laughed when she asked him whether he would ever leave the house at the end of the road. What was it he had said? "I used to be a city boy, but Grandma Ellen loved it out here, and she taught me to love it, too. When your father and mother decided to build close by, that made it perfect." He had thrown his arm around her and pulled her close to him. "I don't have Grandma any more, but I have my family and I have this place. I'm still a lucky man. And I intend to stay right here the rest of my life."

How silly to think he would change his mind for squeaky-voiced Marjorie!

Emily finished her breakfast and went outside, avoiding the backyard where Tony was making dive-bomber noises as he pumped the swing higher and higher. Usually when she wanted to get out from under her parents' eyes, she could go to Christophers' and spend hours with Sally, bicycling, listening to records, or just talking. But Sally was angry with her, and busy besides. She was writing a book. Just to think of it made Emily envious, and being envious of Sally made her feel like a really bad person.

I have to have a project, too, she thought desperately. But what could it be? She couldn't write well or paint, and she hated sewing and cooking except for the batches of cookies she made once a week for her grandfather's cooky jar. Even those had been packaged mixes. What could an envious, ugly, friendless person with no talent do to fill up a summer?

Emily walked to the clearing where she and Tony had talked yesterday and sat down on the same log to think. The woods were steamy after last night's storm. Birdsong filled the air. Emily sat very still, her eyes on a stubby green jack-in-the-pulpit. *This clearing is an island,* she told herself. *I am its princess. The people here are very happy because they've been waiting for years for an Indian princess who wears blue jeans to come and rule them. We're going to live here together for ever and ever.*

Her eyes closed, and she imagined she could hear the voices of the happy people. Then there was laughter, real laughter, and her eyes flew open. Someone was walking along the other path that cut at an angle past this one and went down to the creek. Her grandfather's tall figure came into sight through the trees, and Marjorie was beside him clinging to his arm. As Emily watched, Marjorie stumbled, and they both laughed again.

"—get those walking shoes tomorrow," her grandfather said. "You're going to learn to love this before the summer is over."

Emily let out her breath in a shuddering sigh. When she leaned back to look up at the tree tops, teardrops ran into the corners of her mouth.

If her grandfather only knew how she felt. . . . She stopped crying as she remembered what he always said when she felt sorry for herself. First he would hug her, and then he would say, "If you feel this bad, you'd better do something about it, Emily. You're strong. You're smart. Consider it an opportunity."

Emily blinked the tears away. All of a sudden the answer she needed was there, as clearly as if it were written in the sky above the tips of the birches. She had her project. She had something to do that was important. It was something she could never brag about (like writing a book), but it was really important.

"The name of my project will be Getting Rid of Marjorie," she said out loud for the birds and the jack-in-the-pulpit to hear.

6 · The First Step

"But I don't want to go over to Jimmy's," Tony whined. "I've got things to do here."

"What things?" Emily glared at her brother.

"I'm sorting my matchbooks. Daddy gave me a whole bunch of envelopes, and I'm going to put all the blue matchbooks—"

"You can do that later. Jimmy'll think you don't like him any more."

"I don't need you to take me there, anyway," Tony protested. "Mom doesn't care if I go by myself in the daytime. You just want an excuse to see Sally. I bet you had a fight."

It was really awful to have a little brother who was such a know-it-all.

"I bet you said something mean to her," Tony went on, pleased to have hit home. "Sally never says mean things, but you do, lots of times."

Emily stalked out of his bedroom, slamming the door behind her. It was disgusting to have him be right on all counts. Emily did want an excuse to go to Sally's house, and it was true that she had hurt her friend's feelings. Emily was going to go absolutely crazy if they didn't make up. Sally was the only person she could tell about her project.

Emily's mother was at her desk in the den. "What's the matter, Sweetie?" she said. "You look bored."

"I am." Emily turned away from her mother's cheerful expression.

"Why don't you go over to see your grandfather? He's going to be pretty upset if you don't stop in soon."

"I don't think he's even noticed," Emily snapped. "Besides, he went in to town a while ago. I saw him go by."

Her mother sighed and went back to her work. She did occasional proofreading for a publisher in Milwaukee, and sometimes Emily enjoyed sitting close by and reading over her shoulder. But this was not one of those times. Sooner or later she knew her parents were going to stop suggesting that she visit her grandfather and were going to start ordering her to do it. Her father had almost reached that point already. She wanted to put off the moment as long as possible.

Emily wandered into the living room and scooped Polly out of the playpen. "How's our baby?" she crooned. Polly patted her cheek and chuckled. "Hee," she chirped. "Hee-hee-hee."

Emily put her down and lifted Jane. "Hi, baby," she murmured. "Do you know, you're a pretty nice kid?"

"Hi, yourself." The voice came so unexpectedly and from so close by that Emily almost dropped her squirming sister. Sally stood on the other side of a screened window, peering in at them.

It was the best moment Emily could remember since she

had stepped off the school bus last Friday afternoon. She was so relieved that for a moment she thought she might cry. Instead, she took a deep breath and lifted Jane's tiny hand in a gesture of welcome.

"Come on in," she said unsteadily. "No, I'll come out." She put Jane back in the playpen and dashed to the door. "Have I ever got lots to tell you!"

It turned out that even writers and artists could get tired of doing the same thing all day.

"I have about half the story written down," Sally said proudly. "And I made one drawing, but it was just a practice one. The thing is, I have to be very careful not to get stale." She said this in a way that made getting stale sound mysterious and grown-up, if not desirable. "My uncle says he gets stale if he stays at the typewriter too long. So I thought I'd come over and we could do something this afternoon. If you want to," she added.

Emily nodded eagerly. "I've got a project now, too," she said. "If you want to, maybe you can help me." It was funny how polite they were being to each other. Funny and nice. Making up was so pleasant that it was almost worth getting mad, she thought. Except, of course, if you had only one friend. Then getting mad could be pretty dangerous.

They lay on a blanket under the crab apple tree with lemonade and a box of cookies between them. Emily rolled over on her stomach and pulled at grass blades while she explained what her summer project was.

"You mean you're going to *scare* Marjorie away?" Sally asked, when Emily had finished. She sounded shocked.

"You bet," Emily said. "I'm working on some really great ideas."

"But she already told us she's worried about living here," Sally said. "What if she makes your grandpa move into Milwaukee? That would be awful."

"He wouldn't." Emily closed her eyes for a second, wishing people would stop saying that. "He would never, never leave Chicory Road. He told me so. He's just going to find out what a whiny, crybaby-scaredy-cat she is, and when she decides to go back to Los Angeles, he'll be glad. Wait and see."

"How are you going to do it?"

Emily rolled over on her back again and then rocked to her feet. "I've already started. Come in the garage and I'll show you."

The garage was cool and dim after the bright sunlight of the June day. Emily led the way around her mother's car to the far corner where firewood was neatly piled. She lifted down a carton from the top of the pile and laid it on the top of the car. There was a piece of window screen over the box.

Sally peered in. "Let's see. Oh, yuck! Snakes!" She jumped back in horror.

"One snake," Emily corrected her. "One little grass snake. I had to get up at six o'clock this morning and walk back and forth across the lawn for a half hour before I found it."

Sally retreated to the other side of the car. "What are you going to do with it?"

"I'm going to wait until Marjorie's sitting out on Grandpa's patio, and then I'm going to let it loose. Where she can't miss seeing it. I figure that if she's afraid of the woods she's probably afraid of a lot of other things, too. Like snakes. Most people are afraid of snakes. In fact," Emily said, gaining courage from Sally's presence, "I think I'll do it now. You come with me."

"I don't know. . . . " Sally began, but Emily interrupted impatiently.

"It's a harmless grass snake, for goodness' sake!" she exclaimed. "If she doesn't see one today, she will later on. I just don't want to wait."

Sally looked uncertain, but when she realized she wouldn't have to touch the snake, she decided to go along. She stood guard at the garage door while Emily transferred the captive from its box to a brown paper bag. Then they started down the road, staying just out of sight among the trees that crowded close to the road between the two houses. When they reached the edge of her grandfather's lawn, Emily led the way in a crouching run up the long slope and around the side of the house. Barney saw them and yelped excitedly from his doghouse, but when they disappeared into the tall bushes that edged the west side of the patio, he stopped barking.

Emily crawled on her hands and knees under the hedge, her heart thumping. It was very strange, and not at all pleasant, to approach her grandfather's house as if she were a thief and to look out at the patio where she had played a thousand times and feel she no longer belonged there. The only good part was the feeling she was doing something about her problem. Now, if Marjorie would only come outside!

As if in answer to her wish, the patio door slid open and out she came. She was wearing green again—a terry cloth dress with straps over the shoulders and a yellow daisy on the big patch pocket. Her face was shiny clean and younger looking without makeup, and she wore a yellow towel wrapped like a turban around her head. A tiny white transistor radio hung from a strap around her wrist.

From their hiding place a few feet away, the girls watched as she set the radio on the picnic table and sat down on a bench, her back to the table and the hedge. When she unwrapped her towel-turban and began to dry her hair, Sally giggled so hard that Emily had to poke her in the ribs to silence her.

"But the towel's all streaked with purple! She dyes her hair, Emily."

"Of course she does." Emily hadn't actually realized it before, but now that she saw the evidence she felt as if she had known it all along. Phony, phony, phony, even her hair! Wait till Grandpa found out about that! He might slip once in a great while and say something that sounded phony, but he was still the most honest person Emily knew. Dyed hair, she thought disgustedly, was like living a lie.

"When are you going to do it?" Sally whispered, while a burst of piano music from the transistor rolled across the patio.

"Just about any minute now."

The picnic table, and Marjorie's position with her back to it, were going to make things easy. Emily had worried about whether the snake would crawl in the wrong direction and escape before Marjorie noticed it, but if it was on the table, Marjorie would almost certainly see it when she tuned the radio.

Holding her breath, Emily got up off her knees and moved forward in a crouch. With one quick motion she emptied the contents of the paper bag onto the table, then scuttled back to the bushes.

"You did it!" Sally covered her face with her hands. "Oh, Emily, I can't look."

"Well, I can." Emily pushed aside a leafy branch and peered at the table. "The snake is crawling right toward her back," she whispered. "That's a really great snake. He's doing just what—" She stopped as the snake reached the far side of the table and suddenly disappeared from sight. "Hey, where did he go?"

Sally looked up. "What do you mean, where did he go? He must be right there."

"But he's not!" Emily couldn't believe it. One minute the snake had been following orders perfectly, and the next minute it was gone. Emily moved down toward the end of the hedge.

"Where are you going?" Sally started to get up, but Emily motioned her back.

"I'm going to find out what happened to it," Emily whispered. "You stay there. If the snake comes back this way, you shoo him out again."

Sally looked as if she would rather die.

At the end of the hedge, Emily stood up and brushed off her knees. Then she strolled out onto the patio.

"Hi."

Marjorie jumped. "Emily! Oh, my, you startled me. I didn't know anyone was around." She looked pale under her California tan.

"Sorry," Emily said, her eyes sweeping the patio, the empty picnic table, and the bench. "I just thought I'd stop by and—and see Grandpa."

"Well, that's wonderful," Marjorie said. "He'll be so glad you came, dear."

Dear, Emily thought. That was how California people talked.

"I can't stay," she said. "I just. . . ." Where could the snake have gone?

"But you must wait till your grandfather comes home," Marjorie insisted. "He wants to see you. And I'm delighted to have some company. It's so quiet here. As I told you, I've never lived in such a quiet place. I feel as if there's no one around for miles. That's silly, of course, but if you're not accustomed to it. . . ."

Right then Emily saw the snake. Its narrow green head poked up for just a second above the daisy on Marjorie's patch pocket.

"During that storm the night before last I didn't sleep a wink," Marjorie went on, not noticing Emily's glazed expression. "I kept thinking about how close this house is to the woods and how terrible it would be if one of those big trees was hit by lightning. And I kept hearing strange sounds." She made a little face. "I suppose all this sounds very silly to you."

Emily couldn't speak. She wanted to tell Marjorie that she was right to be afraid, that the country was a very dangerous place in which to live, but her tongue wouldn't work. She couldn't think about anything except the snake curled up in Marjorie's pocket.

And then everything happened at once.

Barney began to bark from his house at the end of the lawn as a car swung into the driveway. Marjorie jumped up and wrapped the towel around her head.

"Is that your grandfather? It must be. Now, where's my lipstick? Oh, he's going to be so happy that you came."

Marjorie's hand dipped into her pocket, and she began to scream. Emily had never heard anyone scream that loud before, not even on television.

The next thing Emily knew, she had been pushed to one side and Grandpa was running across the patio to Marjorie. Pumpkin the cat was just behind him, and they all saw the grass snake at the same moment, wriggling across the stones. Pumpkin pounced and missed, and the snake shot off into the hedge. There was another scream, smaller and squeakier than Marjorie's, and Sally scrambled out onto the patio.

"He came right *at* me!" she moaned. "Oh, Emily!"

"It was in my pocket!" Marjorie shrieked. "Bill, there was a snake in my pocket!" She looked as if she was getting ready to scream again.

Grandpa put his arms around her, not seeming to notice the wet towel and the purplish stains around its edge.

"Everything's all right," he said. "It's gone now. I don't know how it got there, but it certainly won't be back."

"I bet it was crawling around on the table and just dropped down into her pocket," Emily said helpfully. "There are snakes all over the place. I've seen them on this patio lots of times."

Marjorie shuddered and sank down on the bench.

Grandpa looked at Emily with surprise. "You have? I

don't think I've ever—" He gave Marjorie another squeeze and then put out his hand to Emily. "Let's just forget it," he said, "Are you all right, Sally?"

"Yes, Mr. Parker." Sally looked down at her toes.

"Then let's have some lemonade and cookies and talk about something else," he said. "What do you say?"

Marjorie stood up shakily. "Well, yes," she said. "Though I just can't imagine how—"

"Snakes aren't so bad, anyway," Emily said. "I'd rather grab a grass snake than a toad. There're lots of toads around here. Or a shrew. Boy, if you ever had a shrew hiding in your pocket—"

"Emily," Grandpa interrupted. "no more comforting words, please." He grinned at her. "I'm just very glad you girls came to see us."

He put his arm around Emily's shoulders, and she could tell how glad he was. She tried to stay cool, but it was no use. With a sigh, Emily buried her nose in his jacket and breathed the good smell of his pipe tobacco.

"Now that's nice," Marjorie said, her scratchy voice almost back to normal. "Come on, Sally, help me bring out the juice and cookies. You can comb all those twigs and leaves out of your hair. I can't imagine why you picked such a difficult route to the patio."

Over her grandfather's shoulder Emily saw Sally follow Marjorie across the patio. "We were just playing a game, Mrs. Parker," Sally said. She looked back at Emily and scowled. "A pretty dumb game, if you ask me. Emily made it up, but I don't like it. I'm not going to play any more."

7 · Grandpa's Big Announcement

Afterward Emily couldn't remember just how it happened. One minute they were sitting around on the patio drinking apple juice. The next, Grandpa was inviting them all to dinner at the Casa Napoli that night, and a whole list of Italian dishes was running through Emily's mind like a witch's spell. Lasagna, ravioli, rigatoni, spaghetti, pizza— what would she choose? Emily felt Sally's questioning glance and knew she was afraid Emily might refuse to go.

"I guess I can make it," Emily said. "I mean, if Mom says it's okay." That was a laugh. Her mother and father would practically push her out the door if she told them she was going with Grandpa and Marjorie. She just wished she could tell Sally that going out to dinner wasn't going to change anything. She still had her project.

"How about you, Sally?" Marjorie asked.

"I'm pretty sure I can go," Sally said. "I'll call my mom." With her hair brushed and her face scrubbed she looked ready for a party, even though there were some grass smudges on the knees of her pants. She would look ready for a party if she'd been playing tag in a coal bin, Emily thought glumly.

"We'll pick you both up at Emily's house at six," Grandpa said. His narrow, kindly face was so full of pleasure at the thought of the evening ahead that Emily felt uncomfortable meeting his eyes. She knew he had been afraid she would stay away because of Marjorie, and now that Emily was there he was making the most of it. What made it bad was the knowledge that she hadn't come to see him or to be nice to Marjorie but for another reason—one that would have made him unhappy if he had known it.

As Emily expected, her mother was pleased with the invitation. "You'd better take a bath," she said. "And wash your hair. And wear a skirt."

"Sally's wearing pants," Emily said. "I should, too."

Her mother shrugged. "But you look so nice in that brown cotton skirt," she said. *And so fat and awful in pants,* Emily finished for her. But she held firm. She was going to be uncomfortable enough, having dinner with Marjorie. If she wore a skirt she wouldn't even feel like Emily Parker.

Sally settled down with a mystery while Emily went upstairs to bathe and shampoo. Later they sat outside together in the last of the sunlight and Emily toweled her hair dry.

"That's funny," Sally said wickedly. "You have dark hair but you don't have any of that pretty purple color on your scalp." They collapsed against each other, laughing, and Emily thought again how glad she was to have her friend back.

"Marjorie's really not so bad," Sally went on. "When we were in the house getting the juice and cookies, she told me she liked you and wanted to be your friend."

Emily snorted. "How could she like me when she doesn't even know me? She just wants to make Grandpa think she's a good person."

"Maybe." Sally frowned. "But I don't think your project is going to work, Emily. A snake isn't going to make her leave your grandpa and go back to Los Angeles. After all, they *are* married and everything. It's practically a sin to try to make her go away."

"I just wanted to try the snake while I'm waiting to do something else," Emily snapped. "When I get the chance, I'm really going to scare her. You'll see."

Fortunately, Emily's mother called to them right then, putting a stop to their argument. *How can it be sinful if it doesn't feel sinful?* Emily asked herself. She didn't know the answer and didn't want to.

"Your grandfather wants to leave at five-thirty instead of six," her mother said, "so Marjorie can get home in time for a television program she's been waiting to see."

"Probably cartoons," Emily muttered under her breath.

The Casa Napoli was about ten minutes from home. It had a small dining room with thickly plastered walls, clusters of artificial flowers in jelly-glass containers on each table, and candles everywhere. A jukebox played, not too loudly, in the background.

"Not exactly big-city glamour," Grandpa said as Marjorie looked around. "But the food is really good, isn't it, girls?" Emily wished he wouldn't sound apologetic; she thought the Casa Napoli was very romantic.

"I like it," Marjorie said. "It has a nice, homey atmosphere."

Homey! She probably hated it. Emily watched her long pointed fingernails tapping the back of a menu and thought, *She really doesn't belong here.* Marjorie looked like a city person, her black hair swept back to a silky twist and her eyes heavily shadowed. She belonged in a cocktail bar, for goodness' sake, not in a country restaurant. She ought to be grateful to anyone who helped her on her way back to Los Angeles.

"This is great!" Emily's grandfather put out his hands and squeezed Marjorie's wrist and Emily's. "What a lucky fellow I am, out on the town with three lovely ladies!"

"Not half as lucky as we are," Marjorie said. "We have the handsomest escort in the restaurant, haven't we, girls?"

It was really sickening. Emily caught Sally's glance and rolled her eyes, wondering if she could stand a whole evening of such silliness. At their age! The trouble was, her grandfather looked as if he enjoyed that kind of talk. She studied him. Tall and skinny, a thin face, brown eyes with lots of wrinkles around them, gray hair that was always a little bit mussed up, even when he had just combed it. He looked nice, Emily decided, nicer than anybody she knew, but it was really stupid to call him handsome.

"What'll it be, Emily?" he asked. "This is a homecoming party, and the sky's the limit."

She picked up a menu and read down the list of marvels. Spaghetti—too common. Besides, her mother made that, and she was really good at it. Ravioli—possible. Lasagna—better. Rigatoni—perfect! Emily could almost taste the sausage and cheese and pasta drowned in richly flavored sauce.

"Rigatoni," she said. "And garlic bread."

"Terrific. How about you, Sally?"

"Well," Sally said, "I think I'll have the baked chicken."

"The least fattening thing on the menu," Marjorie said. "Wouldn't you know?"

Emily felt her face get hot. "Know what?" she demanded darkly. "Sally doesn't like regular Italian food, that's all."

"No, I don't," Sally said. "I mean, I don't hate it or anything, but I just love chicken." She threw a nervous glance at Emily and hurried on. "I'll have garlic bread, too," she said. "I just love garlic bread."

"Well, that's fine," Marjorie said quickly. "We're going to have just what we want tonight. The lasagna for me, please.' She made it sound as if this was a special extravagance and that tomorrow night and the night after that they had better all eat carrot sticks and cottage cheese. Or, at least, that Emily had better. Marjorie was really a mean woman.

Emily's grandfather didn't seem to be listening. "I'll have the ravioli," he said. "And let's all save room for spumoni. Emily and I are real spumoni addicts, aren't we, Emily?"

Emily felt fatter by the moment. It was as if she were hearing the conversation through Marjorie's ears and looking at herself with Marjorie's critical eyes. Bitterly she remembered the times in the past when she and her grandfather had come here together and gorged themselves on good food and laughter.

They gave their orders. "I suppose you girls have plans for this summer?" Marjorie said. "Why don't you tell us about them."

Emily lowered her eyes, afraid that if she looked at Sally, she'd laugh hysterically. If Marjorie only knew!

"I'm writing a book, Mrs. Parker," Sally said politely. "It's going to be for kids my little brother's age. And I'm drawing the pictures, too. If it turns out okay, I might have it published."

"Why, that's marvelous, Sally! Think of that, Bill. A book! We're going to be glad to say we knew you before you became famous, dear." She was really an awful gusher. And this time Sally was smiling back at her, just as Grandpa had smiled when she had flattered him. Emily wished Marjorie would say something gushy to her, just so she could scowl and ignore it.

"How about you, Emily?" Grandpa asked. "What are you going to do with your vacation?"

I'm going to save you, Emily answered silently. Her grandfather was looking at her, as if he knew that Sally's book depressed her. That was the way he was. If her mother or father caught her being envious of someone, they thought they had to deliver a lecture. Her grandfather never lectured; he knew she felt bad enough already.

"I have some ideas," Emily said carefully. "There's lots of things I can do."

"Good girl."

"Our teacher gave us a reading list for the summer," Emily told him. "Only I've read almost everything on it during the year."

"I'll make a list for you," Grandpa said. "I've been waiting for you to get old enough to enjoy some of the books I've liked best. Maybe this is the summer. What do you think?"

"Great!" Emily said, and meant it.

"My things are being sent from Los Angeles by van," Marjorie interrupted. "When they get here, you may find some books of mine you'd like, too." She paused, and when Emily said nothing, she went on, a little less confidently. "There's one story I've read and reread a dozen times at least. It's about a girl in Shropshire, England, who falls in love with a wonderful man—"

"A love story," Emily muttered. "Yuck."

"It's not an ordinary love story," Marjorie protested. "This girl is a very remarkable person. She has a harelip, and some of her neighbors hate her because they think she's a witch."

In spite of herself, Emily was interested. "I probably won't have time to read it," she said. "Maybe next year." She could always get the title of the book and find it in the library after Marjorie packed up her things and went back to Los Angeles.

The waitress arrived with their orders, and for a while conversation was forgotten. Emily took a bite of garlic bread and closed her eyes in ecstasy. *Someday,* she thought, *I'll write a book myself. It'll be a cookbook, and every single recipe will have garlic in it. Garlic bread and garlic soup, garlic cookies and garlic cake.* The words sang in her head, and she found herself a little less angry with the world. With a sigh of pleasure she turned to the rigatoni steaming in its oval casserole.

When the main course was completed and the plates were replaced with silver dishes of spumoni, her grandfather cleared his throat grandly. "I have an announcement," he said. "Isn't anyone going to ask me what I'm going to do this summer?"

Marjorie's brows drew together in puzzlement. "Gardening?" she asked brightly. "Teach me to be a hiker? Make a book list for Emily?"

"All of that. And as of today, something else." His eyes sparkled, and Emily was amazed to see that he looked almost boyish. "You know I went into town for a meeting with some of the people I used to work with at Carver. They want me to act as consultant on a building project this summer. It's just in the earliest stages, and I'll be making some preliminary drawings and trying to anticipate some of the problems that might come up. I can work at home and just go in once a week or so to talk things over."

"But that's marvelous, Darling!" Marjorie looked as if she were going to hug him. "I *told* you you shouldn't be sitting around just because you've retired. I *told* you your talents are needed. Oh, I'm so pleased!"

Emily made a neat little hole in her scoop of spumoni. She wasn't pleased at all. She thought it was really stupid. Why should her grandfather want to go back to work, even part time, when he didn't have to? Probably he wouldn't have thought of doing it if Marjorie hadn't nagged him about just sitting around. Emily sliced into the ice cream and spooned its soothing creaminess into her mouth. Stupid, stupid, stupid.

"Well, I knew you'd be happy." Grandpa grinned at them all. "There's just one thing about it that you may not like so much. The company's having a kind of retreat up in northern Wisconsin for a couple of days next week. We're all going to sit down and talk about what they want in the new building and what they don't want. There'll be about a dozen people throwing ideas into the hopper. The trouble is, wives aren't invited on this trip. Accommodations are tight, and since we'll be working just about all day long. . . ."

"Oh," Marjorie said in a tiny voice. "Well, that's all right, isn't it? I'll have plenty to do at home getting settled and all."

"You won't mind being alone for a couple of nights?" Grandpa sounded surprised and relieved, and Emily realized why he had picked this time to tell about his new job. He was worried about how Marjorie would feel about being left alone, and he thought she would be less likely to make a fuss in front of others. It was a trick Emily had used many times when she had something unpleasant to confess to her parents.

"What's to mind?" Emily said. "Grandma Ellen used to stay alone lots of times, and she wasn't scared. Not ever."

Marjorie looked pale in the candlelight. "I'm sure I'll get along fine," she said. "It's just something I need to get used to."

"Think of it as an opportunity to get a lot done," Grandpa said. "There'll be nobody to interrupt you." He put his hand on Marjorie's.

Emily swallowed the last spoonful of spumoni. The word "opportunity" rang like a gong in her brain. *Consider it an opportunity* was what her grandfather always said. And here, like a gift, was the best opportunity she could ask for. Scaring Marjorie with a snake had been silly and childish. There were other, much better ways.

"If you want me to, I'll stay with you while Grandpa is

gone," Emily said offhandedly. "I don't mind."

She looked up and then down again hurriedly, to escape three pairs of eyes staring at her in different degrees of astonishment.

8 · A Case of Nosy-itis

Nosy-itis, her mother would have called it. If her mother had known.

There was a scuffling sound in the woods, and Tony bounded out of the underbrush, landing squarely in front of Emily with six-shooters drawn.

"Stop where you are, pardner!"

Emily looked at the skinny little cowboy with annoyance. She had purposely waited till her brother was out of sight, because she didn't want him to know where she was going.

"Scram, pardner. I don't have time to play now."

"This isn't playing." Tony holstered the guns in disgust. "Where're you going?" He paused and answered his own question. "You're going to Grandpa's house. You said we aren't supposed to like Marjorie, but you went out to dinner with her and Grandpa last week, and now you're going to visit them."

"I'm not going to visit them," Emily said, feeling that under Tony's X-ray eye, her nosy-itis was about to become a matter of public record. "I'm just going to look things over. We have to know what's happening."

"Then I'm going with you." Emily used to be able to push Tony around, but not any more. Age was making him difficult.

"Well, come on then, if you have to," she said. "But remember, don't act as if Marjorie's your grandmother just because she lives in that house. Grandma Ellen loved you and made cakes for you and bought you coffee ice-cream cones and played games with you. And she would absolutely hate you if you forgot all about her."

"You shouldn't say 'hate,' " Tony retorted. But he looked uneasy as he fell into step beside her.

"The reason I want to look around," Emily confided, "is because the van came from Los Angeles day before yesterday with all Marjorie's things, and I want to see where she put them. If she changes Grandma Ellen's house one bit, I'll hate her worse than ever."

Tony opened his mouth to protest again but didn't. "I'll help you look," he said. "I'm a very good looker."

As they started up the drive, a motor sputtered in the garage, and a moment later Grandpa appeared riding the tractor mower. He waved to them and gestured toward the house, then swung off over the lawn. He was wearing his grass-cutting cap with the visor pulled low to the tops of his sunglasses. Emily loved the way he rode the tractor, slumped low as if in a saddle, and separated from the world by the drone of the motor and the pleasant monotony of the job.

"Grandpa looks like a cowboy," Emily said. Tony glanced sideways at her as if she were crazy.

They went around to the kitchen door at the back of the

house. Emily considered knocking and then decided not to. She had never knocked on that door in her life. She flung it open and went in. Marjorie, standing at the kitchen sink, dropped a cup with a tiny crash. She looked really annoyed for a second before she managed a welcoming smile.

"Emily. Tony. How nice of you to come visit." She put the handleless cup in the garbage container under the sink and wiped her hands on her apron. "I was just going to fill the dishwasher, but I'd much rather have guests. Would you like some juice or a glass of soda?"

"Soda, please," Tony said, then shot a glance at Emily to see if he was being too agreeable. Emily nodded stiffly and sat down at the kitchen table to look around.

There was plenty to see. The flowered vinyl tablecloth that belonged on the table was gone, and the smooth pine finish was polished to a warm glow. In the center stood a pot of impatiens in full bloom. There were other plants trailing from hanging baskets above the windows.

The counter looked different, too, but for a minute Emily couldn't figure out why. Then she realized that Grandma Ellen's canisters were gone. They had been a gift from Emily and Tony on a long-ago Christmas, and Emily had always loved the pattern of bright daisies and butterflies that covered them. In their place stood a row of apothecary jars, their contents clearly visible. Ugly!

She noticed that Marjorie was watching her.

"This table is going to get all marked up if you don't have a tablecloth on it," Emily said. "Our grandma took very good care of it."

"I know she did," Marjorie said. She brought a tray to the

table with glasses and coasters. "It's a beautiful table—so beautiful that I don't like to keep it covered. But I promise you I'll take very good care of it, too. Would you like some cookies with your soda?"

"Where's the cookie jar?" Tony asked abruptly. "Where's the big teddy bear cookie jar?"

Marjorie looked uncomfortable. "Well, I thought I'd put it away for a while and use this one I brought from Los Angeles." She lifted the cover from a plain square wooden box and scooped out a handful of cookies. "I hope you like peanut butter."

Tony nodded, but Emily wanted to sweep the plate of cookies right off the table. She couldn't believe Marjorie had removed the teddy bear jar. When she was Tony's age she had helped her grandmother pick it out. In fact, she had begged for it even when her grandmother had preferred a plain yellow container with flowers on it. Hiding it away meant that Marjorie thought it was silly and dumb looking and that anyone who liked it was silly and dumb, too.

Emily glanced at the cookies, so precisely ridged and sugared. "I don't eat store-bought cookies," she said. "You never know what's in them."

Emily was a little frightened at her rudeness, but it felt good, too, the way it feels when you've eaten something awful and are finally able to throw up. Marjorie turned very pale, her skin creepy-white against the too-black hair. She sipped coffee from a mug with the initial M on the side. Her eyes were on the liquid, and she kept turning the mug as if she were reading the future in its depths.

"Have you started the list of books your grandfather

gave you?" she asked, finally looking up.

"I finished the one about Mary, Queen of Scots," Emily said. She hoped Marjorie wasn't going to ask a lot of questions; she had enjoyed the book, especially the parts about what life had been like in the sixteenth century, but she had skipped over many of the passages about politics. "I'm going to read *David Copperfield* next."

"That's always been one of my favorites," Marjorie said. "And I loved the motion picture. Freddy Bartholomew, W. C. Fields—but I guess you don't know anything about them, do you?"

"Nope." Wasn't that just like a Los Angeles person to start talking about a motion picture right away? Maybe she hadn't even read the book. Grandpa always looked disapproving when someone said they had seen a movie but hadn't read the book it was based on. And now he had married one of those people!

Tony moved restlessly. He had emptied his glass and eaten three peanut-butter cookies. Now, perhaps because he wanted this visit to be brief, he was ready to move on to another room of the house.

"What else did you bring from California?" he asked. "Besides the cookie jar?"

"Well, lots of books. And some other things." Marjorie stood up and put out her hand to him. "Come on. I'll show you."

She led the way through the dining room, with Tony right behind her and Emily following more slowly. There were other hanging baskets in the dining room, and a pewter tea set stood on the dry sink where Grandma Ellen's crystal candelabrum belonged. A white bowl full of tulips and flanked by yellow candles stood in the middle of the table.

When they stepped into the long narrow living room that stretched across the front of the house, Emily gave a little gasp.

"A piano!" The words slipped out before she could stop them. "You have a piano!" She started toward the small grand that filled one corner of the room, then stopped.

"Would you like to play it?" Marjorie asked. "You're certainly welcome."

"I don't know how."

Just a couple of months ago her grandfather had taken Emily to a piano concert in Milwaukee, and she had decided that she would rather play the piano than do almost anything else. To give recitals wearing a long skirt and a corsage, to play for community singing at school assemblies, to fill the air with thunder or with gentle lullabies depending on her mood—that would be the most wonderful thing in the world. Her father, suspicious of this rather sudden interest, was reluctant to buy a piano, so there had been no point in begging for lessons. How strange that there should be a piano in her grandfather's living room now, when it could do her no good.

Tony ran across the room and touched the keys. "Play a song for us," he said. "Please." He pressed close as Marjorie sat down on the bench and flexed her fingers.

"What would you like?" she asked him.

"Tony's tone-deaf," Emily said venomously. "The only song he can sing is 'Twinkle, Twinkle, Little Star,' and he doesn't do that very well."

Her brother shot her a glance of pure dislike, but she didn't care. Why did he have to give Marjorie a chance to show off?

" 'Twinkle, Twinkle' it is." Marjorie dropped one hand into her lap and with the other picked out the simple notes of the nursery song. *Big deal,* Emily thought. But as the song ended, the other hand came up, and suddenly both hands were moving together, shaping a silky fall of notes, with the tune breaking through each time you thought it was lost for good. Then the ripple of sound faded, and with a crashing of chords 'Twinkle, Twinkle' became hymn-like, bringing goosebumps to Emily's arms. She stood frozen at the doorway, too astonished to move. When the hymn ended, Marjorie gave Tony a little sidewise grin. Once again she played the melody with one hand—the left hand this time—and then her right hand moved up and began a merry race of its own over the upper reaches of the keyboard.

" 'Farmer in the Dell'!" Tony screamed, startled out of his trance. "You're playing two songs at the same time!" He was so pleased with this discovery that when the music ended and Marjorie reached out and hugged him, he didn't protest.

"You make a fine audience," she told him, and then turned to Emily. "Are you sure you don't play?"

Emily shook her head. The piano and the beautiful music had taken her by surprise, but she was over it now. "I was just wondering where Grandma Ellen's love seat is," she said. "It's supposed to be there where you have the piano."

Marjorie's smile faded. "We moved it upstairs to the guest room," she said quietly. "It fits very nicely in the alcove. I'll show you if you like."

But suddenly Emily had had enough. Enough of the changes, big and little, that made this house no longer her own place to love and to criticize. Enough of Marjorie and the piano. Enough of the rough, sharp edges of her own anger that poked through everything she said and did when she was with this stranger in her grandparents' house.

"We have to go," she said. "Come on, Tony. Thanks for the soda." She ran out into the foyer and pulled open the front door without looking back to see if Tony was following.

At the far edge of the lawn Emily stopped running and swept the tears from her eyes. A quick glance showed her that she was alone. Tony was still in the house, and Marjorie was standing at the front door, one hand pressed to her forehead as if she had a pain there.

9 · A Chance to Talk

Emily lay in the sun and let her favorite heaven-dream roll through her mind like a home movie. In it, she was riding in a sleigh, gliding down a twisty, snow-covered road in the moonlight. The speed was breathtaking, the silence total except for the whoosh of wind past her ears. Trees pressed close on either side, the woods were very dark, and she felt happier than she had ever felt before. She could have ridden on forever, but then the trees fell back and the sleigh came to a stop in a clearing. Cozy-looking houses were scattered over the snow, looking like the tiny houses she and her father arranged on a cotton blanket under the Christmas tree each year. Their windows were full of golden light, and smoke spiraled from the little chimneys.

Emily ran to the nearest house and peered in, and there was Grandma Ellen sitting by the fire reading. She looked exactly as Emily remembered her. In the next house was Mr. Clements, the gym teacher who died when Emily was in third grade, and she knew that if she kept looking she would find Elvis Presley, President Kennedy, her great-grandparents, and her mother's brother who died when he was six. They all had their own little houses full of the things they liked best, and the clearing, though it looked small, stretched on forever and ever.

It was a heaven that suited Emily better than the shining city in her illustrated Bible. She thought about it wistfully now, because she was beginning to believe she would never get there. Since the visit to Grandpa's house she had been feeling guilty about her summer project, not because she hated Marjorie less but because the marriage seemed more real to her. She kept thinking about the teddy bear jar packed away somewhere. Its disappearance was a symbol of how things had changed. Perhaps it really was too late to rescue Grandpa from the mistake he had made. Perhaps, as Sally had suggested the night of their dinner at the Casa, it was a sin to try. Still, Emily knew she would go ahead with her project, even if it meant she would never have a perfect little house of her own in the clearing.

The phone rang, and Emily heard her mother answer it in the kitchen. Maybe Sally was calling. Emily almost hoped not. Ever since the night of the dinner there had been a distance between them. When they were together, they talked about Sally's book, or which girls among their classmates were willing to kiss a boy when asked, but not about Emily's project. It had become an uncomfortable, even dangerous subject. Emily groaned, thinking how her one beautiful friendship had been tarnished by Marjorie's coming.

"Emily, it's for you. Grandpa."

Emily rolled to her feet and started to run, then slowed abruptly. This was the first time she had heard from him since the visit, and she was certain Marjorie had told him how rude she was. He could be very stern when he was angry. Still, if he knew, why would he wait two days to scold her? Probably he'd just been too busy going for hikes with Marjorie or packing away Grandma Ellen's things. He probably didn't care what his granddaughter said or did any more.

Emily walked into the kitchen and looked at the telephone for a moment, then shrugged and picked up the receiver. Her mother shook her head reprovingly.

"Emily? How are you doing?" He wasn't angry! "I have to go into town to pick up a few things for the trip tomorrow. Do you want to ride along?"

"Sure." She tried not to sound too eager. "I'll be waiting out in front of the house."

When Emily hung up, her mother came over and stood in front of her with her arms folded. "Your grandfather tells me that you've offered to stay with Marjorie while he's away."

Emily kept her eyes on her mother's diamond ring, admiring the way it sparkled. "Only at night. She's a real crybaby."

"Don't say that. Marjorie's not a crybaby, but she *is* very nervous about living so far from other people. She's heard stories about break-ins and burglaries, and she's worried. It's nothing to be flippant about, Emily. There are lots of problems in big cities like Los Angeles, but somehow country living frightens her more than the city."

"I'm not flippant." Emily tried to look hurt. "I'm going to stay with her, aren't I? Nobody else offered to do that."

"And don't be impudent either." Emily sneaked a look at her mother's face and saw a mixture of doubt and sympathy. "If you're really trying to be a friend to her. . . ."

Emily put her arm around her mother's waist and gave her a squeeze. She felt evil, like Judas or Benedict Arnold, but she had to answer. "Sure, I'm being a friend. I'll kill anybody who breaks in. I'll push him down the stairs. I'll stab him with a toothpick. I'll—"

Her mother laughed. "All right, all right. As long as we understand each other. No funny stuff! Marjorie doesn't expect you to defend her, I'm sure, but it will mean a lot to her just to know someone else is in the house. Your grandfather is really concerned about how timid she is. I told him I think she'll get over it after she's been here awhile and sees how peaceful life is on Chicory Road, but right now she needs all the support she can get. It's too bad Grandpa's meeting had to be scheduled so soon after she got here."

Much to Emily's relief, the car horn brought this painful conversation to a close. She and Grandpa were halfway to the shopping plaza before she began to feel good again. Then the pleasure of being with him chased away her guilt feelings, and she leaned back contentedly. He looked sideways at her and grinned, as if he'd been waiting for this signal that it was all right to talk.

"What's new, Emily? We haven't had much time together, lately. How's Sally's book coming?"

She shrugged. "All right, I guess. She doesn't want me to see it until all the pictures are ready."

"How do you feel about her writing a book?"

Emily was quite sure that he already knew the answer, or he wouldn't have asked the question. But she was glad to talk about it.

"She can do so many things. And besides that, she's beautiful." She paused, thinking about the day her grandfather had come home from California. He had called Emily gorgeous that day, and she had almost hated him for saying something he couldn't possibly mean. Would he say it again now? If he did, she thought, it would be because he had really changed, and they could no longer be honest together.

"Yes," he said. "She's a beauty, all right. And talented, too, from what you tell me. Hard to take, sometimes. Reminds me of my little sister and Shirley Temple."

"Shirley Temple?" Emily frowned. "The old-time movie star? Do you mean your sister knew Shirley Temple?"

Grandpa laughed. "She didn't know her, but she sure did loathe and despise her. Every time Shirley Temple made a new movie, my sister would insist on going to see it. And when she came home from the movie, she'd be grumpy for days afterward. I'd see her glaring at herself in the mirror and brushing her hair around her finger, and trying to tap-dance on the sidewalk in front of our house. I used to tease the daylights out of her. She was so jealous she couldn't see straight."

"You shouldn't have teased her," Emily said. "I feel sorry for her."

He nodded. "I remember once, to make her feel better, my mother told her Shirley Temple would probably grow up to be quite ordinary looking. She told her that lots of times very plain children became beautiful and developed talents as they got older, and child prodigies just faded away."

Emily considered this. "So what happened to Shirley Temple?"

"She grew up into a beautiful woman," Grandpa said with

a grin. "She married a fine man, had a family, was active in politics, worked for the United Nations. She was even an ambassador for a while. My mother certainly didn't call that one right."

"Well," Emily sighed, "that's probably what will happen to Sally, too. She's going to be perfect all her life."

Grandpa put his arm around Emily's shoulder. "The thing is, by the time Shirley Temple grew up, my sister was all grown-up, too. And she turned out to be one of the most interesting people I've ever known. Not movie-star pretty, I guess, but she has the kind of face everyone likes to look at because so much is happening in it. And she can do almost anything she puts her mind to. You ask anybody in Gresham, Kansas, who's the most important person in town, and they'll point to my sister Grace. Everybody loves her in Gresham."

It was a nice story. Emily thought about it while her grandfather was in the drugstore buying shaving lotion and toothpaste. She felt warm and comfortable inside, the way she used to feel when she was with him. It was only when Marjorie was around that he was different. It was terrible to think Marjorie might change him into a Permanent Phony if she had the chance.

When the shopping was finished they went to the Chocolate Drop for milk shakes. They had the best shakes in town —not like the ones Grandpa had when he was a boy, each one made with a quart of milk and a pint of ice cream, but very good, nevertheless. Emily loved the little wrought-iron chairs and round glass tables. If she was careful not to look in the mirror that lined one side of the room, she could imagine herself a slim and dainty girl from the Gay Nineties wearing a wide straw hat with a red ribbon on it. This girl was on the front of the Chocolate Drop menu, and there was something about her—a kind of carefree look—that made you know she could drink chocolate milk shakes every day of her life and never gain a pound.

"I really appreciate your offering to stay with Marjorie while I'm gone," Grandpa said when the waitress had set their shakes in front of them. "She's awfully nervous, but after she's lived here awhile I'm sure she'll get used to it. Anyway, we're much obliged, Emily."

Emily kept her eyes on the thick liquid struggling upward through the red-and-white striped straw. "That's okay," she mumbled.

"Well, it's important to me," Grandpa insisted. "I want Marjorie to be happy here. There are a lot of things we want to do together—travel, for one thing—but I want her to learn to enjoy what's at home, too. We live in about the prettiest place in the world, and I don't want it spoiled for her by a lot of foolish fears."

Travel, Emily thought sourly. That would be Marjorie's idea. Except for the trip to California, Grandpa had been satisfied to stay at home all the time. Now he would probably be on his way to far-off places every week or two, with never a thought for his grandchildren who needed him.

"I'm glad you two will have a chance to get to know each other better," he went on. "She's a wonderful person, Emily. I'd like you to become great friends."

Emily moved the thick, sweet milk around in her mouth. "Umm," she said. Every word he was saying made her more determined to get rid of Marjorie. He wouldn't understand that now, but some day he would look back and thank Emily for caring so much.

When they finished their shakes and went back out into the hot, bright afternoon, Emily felt strong and ready for anything. Grandpa was still Grandpa; Marjorie hadn't been able to change him up to now, and Emily would make sure that she didn't in the future. All the way home Emily sat close to him, her head against his shoulder. When she went into the house, she was smiling.

"Now that's nice to see," her mother said. "I thought those lips had forgotten how to turn up at the corners."

Emily grimaced, then took the scrap of paper her mother held out to her. "What's this?"

"A telephone message from Sally. Something else to smile about, I should think. She wants you to go with her and her family to a lake cottage for two weeks."

"Wow!" Emily looked at the paper. "When?" she demanded. "It doesn't say when."

"They leave next Friday. It's kind of short notice, but they just found there was a cancellation and they can get the cottage they've been hoping for. It's a big one. Sally's mother says you girls will sleep on a balcony." Her mother looked at her expectantly. "Just think, no babysitting for two whole weeks. Aren't you excited?"

"Sure I am," Emily said. But she had to move carefully. This was Saturday. With Friday less than a week away, Emily would have to complete her project in the next few days or take a chance on never being able to do it. After listening to her grandfather talk today, Emily was pretty sure that if Marjorie had another couple of weeks, she would be able to convince Grandpa of anything. If Marjorie tried hard enough, she might even make him move away from Chicory Road.

10 · The "Burglar" Strikes

Except for Grandma Ellen's love seat in the alcove, the blue-and-white guest room looked just as it had before Marjorie moved in. Emily snuggled in the big bed, *David Copperfield* on her chest, and thought about all the times she had slept there when she was little, no older than Tony. She remembered the murmur of her grandparents' voices from the room down the hall, the faraway chime of the clock in the foyer, and the moonlight streaming through the crisp white curtains, just as it was tonight.

Everything was peaceful in the olden days, Emily thought. Now her stomach churned and her head throbbed. She wanted to pray her childhood prayer. "Now I lay me down to sleep," but the words didn't come. When you were about to do something wicked, it was useless to pray. Besides, Emily was not laying herself down to sleep. Just the opposite. She had to stay awake until Marjorie was in bed.

It had been an uncomfortable evening. Emily's father had walked over with her at nine o'clock, and they had found the shades drawn and the screen door locked. Barney was inside,

barking furiously, while Marjorie peered out and then unlocked the inside door and the screen.

"Well, you seem to be ready for anything," Emily's father
said. "Fort Knox could take lessons."

Marjorie smiled uneasily, as if she suspected she was being
laughed at. She offered them coffee, milk, and cookies and
looked disappointed when Emily's father said he had to go
home and do paper work. Clearly, she wanted company, the
more the better.

As soon as he left, Emily had announced that she would
watch her favorite comedy hour on television and then go to
bed.

"Well, that's fine," Marjorie said. "You do whatever you
want to do." But again she looked disappointed, and Emily
saw her glance at the checkerboard and a deck of cards that
had been lying on the coffee table. In spite of herself, Emily
remembered times at school when she had tried to be friendly
with a girl at the next desk or had joined a couple of people
who were talking in the hall, only to have them suddenly stop
talking and walk away. You always knew when you didn't
belong. Marjorie knew.

Promptly at ten, Emily said good night and went upstairs.
She had a paper bag containing pajamas, extra underwear,
toothbrush, comb, two Milky Way bars, three cookies, *David
Copperfield,* three empty beer cans, a pliers, and a long piece
of wire folded into twelve-inch lengths. She was counting on
the candy and cookies to keep her awake until Marjorie went
to bed.

The food was all gone, and *David Copperfield* had tumbled
over on Emily's chest twice, with a rib-cracking thump each

time, before she finally heard footsteps in the hallway and the sound of the bathroom door closing and opening again. When the hall light went off, Emily pushed the book aside and slipped out of bed. It was time.

Emily wished Sally were here, though, of course, Sally would probably refuse to help. Still, she would be company. At home there was always the sound of the television or stereo downstairs, her father's breathy little whistle, the refrigerator door opening and closing, her mother coming down the hall on tiptoe to check on the twins. Here the silence was complete, except for an occasional June bug thumping against the screen.

Emily sat crosslegged on the carpet and used her father's pliers to straighten the wire. At either end she shaped a hook, then tied her sneaker laces to one of them, using three or four knots to make sure they wouldn't slip. Her hiking boots would have worked better, but her mother would have asked why she was wearing hiking boots to walk a couple of hundred feet down the road.

The next step was to remove the screen from her window. That was easy. Emily had helped her grandfather many times to exchange the screens for freshly washed storm windows. She switched off the lamp so the June bugs wouldn't fly in and leaned out the window to throw the empty beer cans out on the lawn. Then she was ready to lower the wire.

There was a tall clump of forsythia just below, and Emily had to be careful to avoid tangling the sneakers in the branches. When the shoes were dangling outside the den window, Emily began whipping the wire in a narrow arc so that the sneakers bumped against the screen.

With the third thump, there was a small, questioning yip from Barney, who usually slept in the hallway just outside the den. Then came a whole series of excited barks. Emily let the sneakers scrape across the screen once or twice, and the barking turned frenzied.

"Emily! Are you awake?"

Emily hooked the wire over the windowsill and ran to the door. She opened it just a crack.

"Someone's trying to break in, Emily." Marjorie's voice was even scratchier sounding than usual. "Listen to Barney! I'd better call the sheriff."

Emily opened the door a little more and slipped out into the hall.

"It's probably nothing," she said. "Barney barks at nothing sometimes. Maybe he heard an owl." Emily sounded as if she were trying to convince herself. "I'll go downstairs and see."

"No, you mustn't!" Marjorie gripped her arm fiercely. "If there's someone down there—"

The barking stopped. After a full minute of standing in the dark, Emily felt Marjorie's fingers relax.

"You're sure he barks at owls sometimes?"

"I *think* so."

Marjorie went to the top of the stairs. "Barney?" Her voice quavered. "Here, Barney."

"You'd better not call him upstairs," Emily said. "If there *is* a burglar, it's better if Barney's down there."

"I suppose you're right." There was movement at the foot of the stairs, and the big dog appeared in the moonlight, looking up at them.

"Good boy," Marjorie called. "Good boy. You stay there." She turned back to Emily. "I don't know what to do," she said childishly. "This is terrible."

"I'm pretty sure it was just an owl he heard," Emily said. She went back to her bedroom and closed the door behind her, leaving Marjorie at the top of the stairs.

The project was underway.

Emily braced the screen against the window to keep out insects and then climbed back into bed. It was only twelve-thirty. With a sigh she opened *David Copperfield* again. It would have been smarter to bring an exciting mystery, she thought, and she certainly should have packed more cookies. Staying awake was going to be the hardest part of the project.

When Emily's watch said one-thirty, she lifted the screen from the window and began swinging the wire again. This time it took Barney longer to respond; he must have been deep in sleep. But when he finally did hear the noise at the window, he woke with a roar. Emily barely had time to jump back into bed before her door opened.

"Emily! Emily, are you awake?" Marjorie actually sounded as if she were crying. "Barney's going crazy down there. I really do think I should call the sheriff."

Emily tried to sound sleepy. "Maybe he had an exciting dream," she said. "Maybe he thought he was chasing a rabbit. Something like that. See, he's starting to calm down already."

"Oh, I hope you're right." Marjorie stood, halfway into the room. "I thought having Barney in the house would make me sleep better, but this barking—"

Emily closed her eyes and gritted her teeth. *One, two,*

three, out you go, she thought. The door closed, and there was the sound of soft footsteps going back down the hall.

After that the project slowed down because Emily fell asleep. She had planned to waken Barney every hour, but it wasn't until four o'clock that a bad dream woke her up. Why, it was practically morning! The birds had begun their songs in the almost-dark.

This time Barney must have been awake and wandering around the house. At the first thump of the sneakers against the window, he started to bark. Hurriedly, Emily pulled up the wire and carried it to the closet. Something was wrong. The wire felt different. Emily reached for the hook, but the sound of Marjorie's voice made her panic, and she thrust the wire deep into the closet. Then she fastened the screen in place and dashed back to bed. Barney continued barking, as if this time he wouldn't stop till he caught the intruder.

Seconds ticked by. Had Emily imagined Marjorie's voice down the hall? When she could bear the suspense no longer, Emily slipped out of bed and opened the bedroom door. The hallway was dark, but at the other end a narrow frame of light outlined Marjorie's door. Emily tiptoed down the hall.

"Nineteen hundred Chicory Road. The last house. Please hurry! Yes, yes, I will!"

She was calling the sheriff! Emily shivered. She had known this might happen, but now that it had, she didn't know whether to be pleased or worried. Could you go to jail for trying to frighten someone? What if there was some special kind of guilty look that a policeman would recognize?

Emily opened the bedroom door, and Marjorie screamed. "It's me! Emily!"

Marjorie pulled her into the room. "I've called the sheriff," she gasped. "They said to stay upstairs till they get here." She was fully dressed in blouse and slacks, with a scarf knotted around her hair. Her face was white and old looking in the pale light of a lamp.

Emily looked at the unopened bed.

"I was sitting up reading when Barney barked the first time," Marjorie whispered. "I just didn't bother to go to bed after that. I knew I wouldn't sleep. And there *is* a prowler, Emily. There has to be. You may not think so, but that dog is very upset about something. I should have called the sheriff hours ago. Maybe I should call your father, too."

"Oh, no!" The words were out before Emily could stop them.

Marjorie nodded. "I suppose you're right. I certainly don't want anything to happen to him. If there's someone down there with a gun—" Her voice rose hysterically.

"I'd better get dressed." Emily started for the door, but Marjorie seized her wrist and drew her back into the circle of light. "No! You stay here till the sheriff comes," she said. "We have to stay together."

Marjorie ran to the window, pulling Emily behind her. A half-mile away a blinking red light moved along the highway, hesitated, then turned down Chicory Road.

"Thank goodness!" Marjorie exclaimed. "I couldn't bear this much longer!"

The red light winked into the driveway, and Barney went crazy.

"I'm going to get dressed," Emily said again. She broke away and ran down the hall to the guest room. Underwear, shorts, shirt—shoes! Her sneakers were still tied to the wire!

Emily crawled to the closet and felt inside. She found one sneaker, loosened the knots, put it on, and reached for the other. Her hand slid along the wire to its end. The sneaker wasn't there.

"I'm going downstairs," Marjorie called softly. "You can stay up here if you want to, Emily. We'll be safe now."

But of course she wasn't safe. She had to find the sneaker. Frantically, Emily ran her hands over the closet floor. It was bare. She remembered then that the wire had felt different— lighter?—when she pulled it in the last time. That was it, the only possible explanation. The sneaker was lying right below the bedroom window where the sheriff's men would find it.

Emily could almost hear the conversation.

"Whose sneaker is this?"

"Find the owner and you find the prowler."

"I'd say it belongs to a girl, eleven or twelve years old. . . . You have any eleven-year-old girls around here, Mrs. Parker?"

Emily moaned and ran to the window. She looked out into the mist. Figures with flashlights were moving across the lawn toward the house. From her right came the sounds of locks being opened, and then a rectangle of light from the foyer spilled across the lawn. The two policemen went up to the door, and Emily could hear their low questions and Marjorie's scratchy-voiced replies. The door closed, and the policemen moved toward the bushes below the bedroom window.

Emily ran back to bed and pulled the sheet up to her nose. At any moment they would find her sneaker, and she would be disgraced forever. Facing the policemen's questions would be bad enough, but what would her parents say when they found out? And Grandpa! He would never forgive her. Never. Why hadn't she used something else instead of her sneakers to make a noise? Why had she started the project at all? Wickedness was always punished. Why had she thought she could get away with it?

The policemen moved around the side of the house. Emily could follow their progress by listening to Barney's barks as he moved with them from window to window. By the time they had worked their way all around and were back at the front door talking to Marjorie again, Emily felt sick. *When they ask me if it's my shoe, I'll probably throw up,* she thought. *Yuck!*

Emily was curled up in a tight ball, clutching her stomach, when the voices stopped and the front door closed. Moments later Marjorie came into the guest room and sat at the foot of the bed.

"Well," she rubbed her forehead wearily, "they've checked all the bushes and under the windows and—" She paused as though she could hardly bear to say the words. "There really was a prowler!"

"There was?" Emily looked down and saw that her single sneaker made a peculiar lump under the sheet. She pressed her foot flat. "Do the police want—I mean, do I have to go downstairs?" Emily's throat felt furry.

"No, I don't think there's anything more we can tell them. You see, they found beer cans out on the lawn! Your grandfather doesn't drink beer, and I don't, and if we did, we certainly wouldn't leave the cans lying around outside. So there really was someone here, walking around, drinking beer and trying to find a way to get in."

"Did the police—" Emily's voice was a squeak. "Did they find anything else?"

"They're still looking." Marjorie touched the goose bumps on her arms. "They've gone over to your house to look now. Whoever it was may have gone from house to house trying to find an open window or an unlocked door. Isn't that a terrible thought?"

Marjorie bent her head, and when she looked up she seemed to have made up her mind about something. "I want to tell you this, Emily. It happened when I was a little girl, only about a year older than Tony is now. It's something I don't like to talk about. In fact, I haven't even told your grandfather. I suppose I thought that at some point in my life I could leave it behind. But I don't believe I can."

Marjorie massaged her forehead again and then hurried on, not looking at Emily as she talked. "I was staying with my aunt and uncle one summer. My uncle was a game warden, and he and my aunt lived in a cottage at a beautiful lake in the north woods. It was supposed to be a great treat for me, but I'd never been away from the city before. The woods, the strange night noises, the loneliness—I just couldn't get used to it.

"One night my aunt was visiting friends, and my uncle got a telephone call to come to his headquarters right away. There was some kind of emergency. I heard him tiptoe to my door and look in, and then I heard him go outside and get into his car and drive off. I never felt so alone in my life."

Emily squirmed. "He shouldn't have left you."

"Well, he thought my aunt would be home very soon. And he loved that lake and the cottage and the forest. I don't think he believed that anyone *could* be afraid there or that anything bad would ever happen there. . . ." Marjorie pulled her knees under her like a little girl. "I lay there in bed, too terrified to move, and after a long time there was a sound at the window. I looked, and it was all my worst dreams rolled into one. A man was coming through the window. He went past my bed like a shadow. For what seemed like hours—but it was really only minutes—he was out there in the cottage, taking what he wanted. I was sure he would kill me before he left, if I didn't die of terror first. Then he came back into the bedroom and went to the window and climbed out. And he was gone. I don't think he ever noticed me, or if he did he was convinced that I was sound asleep. We found out later that he'd been waiting for a chance to break in because my uncle had a lot of valuable radio equipment."

Marjorie closed her eyes as though she was trying to shut the memory away, then opened them and looked at Emily. "And that's why I'm such a scaredy-cat now," she said. "Nothing happened, really, and I pretended to forget about it because my uncle and aunt felt so bad. But I never have forgotten it. When I'm alone, I feel as helpless as I did then. I've always wanted lots of people around me, and when I moved into my own apartment I had bars on the windows and special locks. When your grandfather and I decided to get married and move back here, I thought, 'It'll be all right now. I'm a big girl.' But I guess I'm not. Tonight I was that terrified little girl all over again."

Emily realized that somewhere during this story she had

stopped breathing. Her chest ached. Morning light poured through the windows, but she could imagine, all too clearly, a dark shadow stepping over the sill. *All my worst dreams rolled into one.*

"Well!" Marjorie gave the bed a sudden brisk tap and stood up. "Enough of that. The sheriff's men have promised to check back tonight, three or four times, just in case the prowler returns. And tomorrow night your grandfather will be home, and we can talk about all this together. Right now I'm going downstairs to fry some bacon and eggs for us and give Barney a whole handful of dog biscuits. He's earned them." She smiled anxiously at Emily. "You will stay for breakfast, won't you?"

Emily nodded. "I'll be down in a minute."

When Emily was alone, she got up, took off her sneaker, and pushed it to the bottom of her paper bag. Then she took the wire from the closet and folded it up. She made the bed, puffing the pillows the way she never bothered to do at home. When the room was in order, she sat down on the edge of the bed, where Marjorie had sat, and curled her bare toes in the carpet.

Emily felt terrible. She felt worse than terrible. And that was strange, since the project was working. Marjorie was scared to death. She was almost certainly going to tell Grandpa tomorrow night that she wanted to go back to where there were lots of people around and bars on the apartment windows. She was practically on her way to Los Angeles.

Then why do I feel so awful? Emily wondered. *Why do I*

want to pull the covers up over my head and hide for all the rest of my life?

Whatever was wrong, it was a lot worse than the problem of a missing sneaker.

11 · The Missing Sneaker

"If I'd been there I would have caught him!" Tony slid a six-gun from its holster and aimed from a skinny hip. "This looks like a real gun, right? I'd have kept him up against the wall until the sheriff got there."

Emily sighed. Ever since Tony had heard Marjorie's version of the night's adventure, he had been furious because he had missed the excitement. He was already insisting that he was going to protect "the girls" the second night.

"You're a male chauvinist pig," Emily told him. "Girls can protect themselves. We managed, didn't we?"

"You didn't catch the burglar. But I will! Just wait. When Marjorie and I get back from town, she's going to show me where the beer cans were lying and—"

Emily had started out of the room, but she turned back. "You're going to town with her?"

"She has to get groceries and she asked me if I wanted to ride along and get an ice-cream cone," Tony said casually. "I can't help it if she likes coffee ice-cream cones as much as I do. It doesn't mean I'm forgetting Grandma Ellen. It just means Marjorie is nice, too."

Emily glared and turned away. She was tired, more tired than she'd ever been in her life. She felt as if she hadn't slept at all last night. And she was worried, too. Tony's excitement about the "prowler" was predictable, and her mother had been surprised and frightened. It was her father's reaction that made her uneasy. He listened to Marjorie's story, but all the time she was talking he looked at Emily. *With question marks in his eyeballs,* she thought.

"That was a pretty persistent prowler," her father said mildly, when Marjorie sat back, her story at an end. "Strange that he would stay around for hours."

"It was just awful," Marjorie agreed. "A nightmare." She, too, looked exhausted.

"I'm so sorry it happened while Dad Parker was away," Emily's mother said. "What a dreadful coincidence!"

Her father nodded, his eyes still on Emily. "Yes, quite a coincidence." He picked up his suit jacket from the back of his chair. "I have to get down to the office, but we can talk about it some more this evening. Maybe you should come over here to sleep."

"Oh, I think we'll be all right tonight," Marjorie told him. "I don't want you to bother yourselves about this. The sheriff's men are going to come around several times—and, anyway, I don't think a burglar would come back the second night in a row, do you? I mean, he probably realizes that even if he found a loose window, he wouldn't be able to get in without arousing Barney."

Tony looked disappointed. "He might," he said. "You'd better let me stay with you tonight, Marjorie. I'll bring my gun with me."

"You'll stay right here, my boy." His father roughed Tony's hair. "Marjorie doesn't need a second protector, does she, Emily?"

Once again, Emily felt her father's look, like a knife. She wished for the thousandth time that he would say what he was thinking instead of making sarcastic comments.

When her father had left for the office, and Marjorie and Tony had gone to town, Emily helped her mother clean up the kitchen and give the babies their baths. Then she hurried outside and headed down the road to her grandfather's house. Her head throbbed, and she would have liked to go upstairs to her own quiet room to sleep, but she had to find the missing sneaker. Even if it stayed lost and no one else discovered it, she knew she would be in trouble; sooner or later her mother would want to know why she was wearing her old sneakers with the worn-through toes.

As Emily crossed the lawn, Barney barked joyfully from his doghouse. He didn't sound at all fierce in the morning light, just pleased to see her. *Even he would hate me if he knew what I did last night,* Emily thought. If the truth came out, she wouldn't have a friend left.

Emily went to the corner of the house and crawled behind the shrubbery. If the sneaker had flown off while she was swinging the wire, it might have traveled a long way. She pushed aside leaves and twigs, almost putting her hand on a partly buried toad. He blinked in annoyance at this strange visitor, then hopped away. Emily crawled on, getting more panicky by the minute. The sneaker had to be there someplace, but it wasn't.

When she reached the clump of forsythia, Emily sat down and leaned back against the house. The den and guest-room windows were above her, out of sight. Overhead, a sweep of leafy branches made a sunlit tent, sweet smelling and private. Emily closed her eyes for a moment and pretended she was on her wooded island again, a thousand miles from Chicory Road. It was the same dream she dreamed at school once in a while—a magical leap far from girls who didn't want to be friendly and boys who called her Tubby. On bad days she had sometimes stayed on the island for hours at a time, hearing her teachers but not really listening, a slim and beautiful Indian princess who did good deeds and was loved by everyone.

"Emily, are you there?" The whisper came from very close by.

Emily's eyes flew open. The branches had parted, and Sally's golden head appeared in the opening.

"What are you *doing* in here, Emily? Are you hiding from someone?"

Of all the people Emily knew, Sally was the only one she would have wished to see right then. "I'm looking for something," she said. "It's in here and I have to find it."

"With your eyes closed?" Sally crawled into the forsythia-tent and dropped something in Emily's lap. It was the missing sneaker.

Emily looked at her friend unbelievingly. Sally was a real princess, the one who made everyone happy. "Oh, thanks!" she exclaimed. "Thanks a million times! Where did you find it?"

"Stuck in the yew bush back there." Sally settled herself

against the wall. "I was on my way to your house when I saw you crossing the lawn, so I cut through the woods and came out just as you were crawling into the bushes. I don't understand, Emily. How did your sneaker get caught in a yew? And why do you look so funny? Have you been crying?"

Emily rubbed a grimy hand across her eyes. The need to talk to someone about what had happened was great, but she hated to face Sally's disapproval.

"It's my summer project," she said finally. "You know—getting rid of Marjorie." She shot a glance at her friend and then looked away. "It isn't working. I mean, it *is* working, but I feel awful. You were right," she went on humbly. "It was a terrible idea. And I wish I'd never thought of it." She waited for her friend's I-told-you-so.

"What exactly did you do?" Sally asked. She reached over and squeezed Emily's hand. "You didn't throw your sneaker at her, did you?" She giggled, and Emily sighed.

"I'll tell you," she said, and as quickly as possible she described the events of the night before. Sally listened without comment, a wondering expression on her face as she stared at the sneaker in Emily's lap.

"So you see," Emily finished, "she really has a good reason to be afraid. I'd be afraid of being alone, too, if something so horrible had happened to me when I was little. She says she can't ever get over being scared. I'm pretty sure she's going to tell my Grandpa that she's going back to Los Angeles."

Sally squeezed her hand again. "But it's what you wanted, isn't it?"

"That's the trouble," Emily groaned. "I *do* want her to go

away so that everything can be the way it was before, but I *don't* want to be the person who makes her go. I feel just ghastly every time I think about last night."

"Well, maybe she won't leave," Sally said. "Maybe your grandfather will talk her out of it."

"And maybe pigs have wings," Emily said mournfully. "You didn't see her face, so you don't know how frightened she was. The only thing that would make her feel better would be for me to tell her that I was the prowler—and I'd rather kill myself!"

"Oh, Emily."

They sat in silence for a few moments, and then Emily changed the subject.

"Have you finished your book?"

Sally's pretty face turned glum. "I don't even want to talk about it," she said bitterly. "You're not the only one who picked the wrong project for this summer."

"What do you mean?"

"My uncle came over for dinner last night—the uncle I told you about who knows all the editors. I showed him the story and the pictures that were finished, and he said—" Her voice cracked with outrage. "He said they were pretty good for a child."

"Oh, that's mean!" Emily exclaimed, forgetting her own troubles for a moment. "I hate it when grown-ups—"

"He said there was no use showing it to an editor because they see hundreds of manuscripts from *children,* and they're never good enough to publish. He said it was good experience for me, and I should keep trying." Sally sighed pitifully. "All that work for nothing! I was going to throw the whole thing into the fireplace, but my mother wouldn't let me."

Emily struggled with an unpleasant mix of feelings. Here was her dearest friend, practically her only friend, telling her how unhappy she was. *Why can't I feel sad for her, the way she feels sad for me? How can I be even a little bit glad that her book won't be published?* It was further proof, if proof was needed, that Emily Parker was a first-class rat.

"I'd like to read your book," Emily said. "And I'll bet Mrs. Gardner will think it's great when we go back to school in September. She'll probably put it on display in the library. You'll be the only person who wrote a book during summer vacation."

Sally looked at her thoughtfully. "Why, I never thought of that, Emily," she said. "I *could* take it to school, I guess."

"And some day you'll write another one and it will be published," Emily said. "I just know it." The pleasure in her friend's face made her feel slightly less guilty about her own feelings.

A rustling in the bushes interrupted the conversation. The cat Pumpkin glided into the forsythia-tent and stared at them.

"We'd better get out of here," Emily said. "I don't want to be crawling out of the bushes with a sneaker in my hand when Marjorie comes home."

"Let's forget all this bad stuff and go over to my house," Sally suggested. "We can make lists of what we're going to take to the cottage."

Emily followed Sally out of the shrubbery on hands and knees, then ran with her across the lawn and into the woods. She did want to forget all the bad stuff for a while, but it wasn't going to be easy. With the sneaker recovered, no one was going to find out what she had done, but somehow that didn't make her feel much better.

It would be great if you could go away to a lake cottage and leave your conscience at home.

12 · Emily Attacks

"You don't have to walk with me," Emily said. "It isn't even dark yet."

"But I want to," her father said. "I need the exercise. And besides, we can't have a wicked burglar stealing our little girl."

"I want to go, too," Tony whined. "I want to stay at Grandpa's house and take care of Marjorie." He was poised at the door, his six-guns riding so low on his hips that Emily wondered how he could walk. Ever since Tony's return from town, he had been repeating his offer of protection and becoming increasingly annoyed because no one took it seriously.

Now their father patted his shoulder and gave him a little push away from the door. "Marjorie doesn't need two protectors," he said. "And she only has one guest room. She'd have to make up a bed for you on the couch, and there's no reason to put her to all that trouble."

"She wouldn't care. She said so."

But the battle was lost and Tony knew it. Emily felt sorry

for him and wished he were coming along. She didn't want to walk alone with her father, and she dreaded the evening with Marjorie. All day she had been torn between two possibilities. First, it might be that no one would ever find out what she had done. Marjorie might just tell Grandpa she was afraid to live in the country and the marriage was a mistake. She would move back to Los Angeles, and everything would be the way it was before, except, of course, that Emily's conscience would torture her for the rest of her life. Second, she could confess—tell the whole story to her family and apologize to Marjorie. Then she would be in disgrace, and Grandpa would belong to Marjorie forever.

There wasn't much of a choice, she thought sourly, following her father out the door. It was the kind of problem she would have talked over with her grandfather, but this time he was right in the middle of it. There was no one except Sally, and so far Sally hadn't made her feel any better.

It was a perfect summer evening. The sun had slipped behind the trees, leaving a pale, silvery light that made Emily feel as if she were walking through water. *If Marjorie stayed for one summer she would learn to love this,* she thought and then pushed the idea angrily away.

"Are you nervous about tonight, Emily?"

Emily looked up at her father. He *was* teasing her; she was sure of it. What did he know? What did he suspect?

"Not really," she said carefully. "I don't think there's anything to be nervous about."

"Neither do I. Although it's true that there have been some break-ins in the neighborhood in the last week. Not on Chicory Road, but less than half a mile away."

"There were?" Emily stared at him in surprise. "Real burglars?"

Her father nodded. "Real burglars. But I don't think we need to tell Marjorie about that. Somehow I don't think it was *that* burglar who was keeping you both awake last night."

He looked at Emily expectantly, but Emily turned her face away. She needed time to think, and her father wasn't giving it to her. She could feel him wanting her to confess. They cut across Grandpa's wide front lawn in silence, and when the front door opened to welcome them, Emily found herself almost glad to see Marjorie standing there. For the moment, at least, her father would stop talking about last night.

"Now this time you *must* come in for a few minutes." Marjorie waved Emily inside and took her father's wrist to draw him into the house. "I've made some cocoa, and if you'd rather have lemonade, I have that, too. And oatmeal cookies. Everybody likes oatmeal cookies, I guess. I hope! Come along, Emily. You can put the cookies on a plate while I pour the drinks." Marjorie was talking so fast that no one else had to say anything. They followed her into the kitchen, and when the cookies and cocoa were on the table they sat down obediently and ate. Emily felt as if she might choke.

She glanced at her father and saw that he was uncomfortable, too. "Very good cookies," he said. "Oatmeal is my favorite. Followed by chocolate chip, peanut butter, and any other kind of cookie in the whole world."

Marjorie laughed. "Oh, that's fine," she said in her scratchy voice. "I'm not much of a baker, but cookies are fun. I'm practicing." She smiled at Emily.

As soon as her father's cocoa cup was empty, he stood up. "I'll have to leave you now, ladies," he said. "Tony will never forgive us if he thinks we had a party without him." He looked at Marjorie and then at Emily. "You have a good sleep," he said. "I don't think you're going to have any more problems, and Emily agrees with me. Don't you, Emily?"

She nodded stiffly. He might as well come right out with his suspicions instead of hinting this way. Marjorie smiled at them both. It was a small, unhappy smile, guaranteed to make a guilty person feel worse than ever. In spite of herself, Emily smiled back.

Actually, the evening wasn't as painful as Emily had thought it would be. Marjorie had the checkerboard out again, and they played three games. It was fun, even though Marjorie won each time.

"You're really good," Emily said, after her third loss. "I can beat my grandpa, but I can't beat you."

"I usually beat him, too," Marjorie said. "And it doesn't bother him at all. He doesn't mind being beaten by a woman —that's one of the things I love about him."

"Why should he care if it's a woman who beats him?" Emily demanded. She had never heard anything so silly.

Marjorie arranged the checkers neatly in their box. "A lot of men do care, Emily. You'd be surprised. I had a friend I used to play tennis with quite often, and sometimes I'd let him win a couple of games, just so his day wouldn't be spoiled."

"I'd never do that," Emily declared hotly. "I'd never *let* someone else win if I could play better."

"And that's one of the many things that's special about

you," Marjorie said, smiling. "You're honest right to your toes. How about some popcorn?"

They went out to the kitchen and popped corn together, and then Marjorie played the piano for a while. Emily sat with her book in her lap and a bowl of popcorn at her side.

Honest to my toes, Emily thought. *What a joke that is!* She forced herself to stop thinking about anything but the music. When Marjorie played, she made it sound like the most fun in the world. Tonight she was playing show tunes, moving from one familiar melody to another without a break. Emily closed her eyes and dreamed of a party she would go to some day in the future. She would be chic and graceful, and when someone said, "Let's sing," she would sit down at the piano and play whatever they wanted. The other guests would group themselves around her, singing and laughing and having a great time because their friend Emily was playing for them. "Now play a solo," they would beg, and everyone would stop talking as her fingers flew over the keyboard and beautiful music filled the room.

"Emily. Emily?"

It was Marjorie, shaking her gently.

Emily opened her eyes. "I could learn," she said, still caught up in her dream.

"Learn? To play the piano?"

"I was dreaming," Emily said hastily. "I'm pretty tired, I guess. I'd better take a shower and go to bed."

"You go right ahead. I'm going to check the doors once more, and then I'll be up, too." Marjorie walked with Emily to the foot of the stairs. "It's been fun having you here," she said, so softly that Emily, hurrying up the stairs, could pretend not to hear. Still, the scratchy little voice and too-eager smile seemed to follow her right into the bathroom.

When Emily came out, twenty minutes later, the lights were still on downstairs. She hurried to the guest room and jumped into bed without turning on the lamp. Soon she heard the door open softly.

"Emily? Good night, Emily."

Emily lay very still, and when she peeked at last, Marjorie was gone, leaving the door open a crack. Emily felt more alone than she ever had in her life. *This is how it'll be from now on,* she thought. *Just me and my terrible, rotten, mixed-up thoughts.* When she slept, finally, she dreamed again that she was playing the piano. This time when she touched the keys they made a snarling sound.

The clock in the foyer was chiming four when she sat up, wide awake. What was it that had startled her? Was it the ugly sound in her dream? No, it was something else, a snarl that was continuing right now. Barney was snarling downstairs, a deep and terrifying growl far worse than a bark.

Real burglars! Emily could hear her father's voice saying the words. Something had to be happening downstairs to make Barney growl like that.

Emily slid out of bed and tiptoed across the room and down the hall. The bathroom door loomed on her right, a pale rectangle in the pre-dawn light. Emily remembered a can of hairspray standing on the shelf. It would have to do for a weapon. She found it and started down the stairs on tiptoe, too frightened to breathe.

The growling came from the kitchen. Emily crossed the dining room and peered around the corner. Barney was in the middle of the room, crouched almost flat and staring at the door. What did he hear? Emily waited, then moved across the linoleum to stand beside him, the can of hairspray pointed at the door.

The doorknob turned.

"Awwwkkkk!" Emily's scream came right from her toes as a dark figure came through the doorway. Frantically she pumped the hairspray, screaming again and again, "Get him, Barney! Get him! Get him!"

Barney launched himself in a long jump that took him to the man's shoulders. The figure staggered backward, and Emily reached with one hand for the knife rack over the counter while with the other she kept spraying. The intruder crashed to the floor.

"Emily! Emily, is that you? Down, Barney, down! Stop it, Emily! No more!"

Emily stopped, aware that Barney's growls had changed to joyful yelps. The figure in the back hall was getting up, coughing and choking, its shape suddenly familiar.

"Grandpa!"

Emily ran into his arms, letting the spray can and the butcher knife clatter to the floor. "Oh, Grandpa, I'm sorry! Oh, I'm sorry! Grandpa, I might have killed you!"

The kitchen light went on, and Marjorie appeared, clutching her robe around her.

"Bill, Emily, are you all right? Good heavens, what's happening?"

Grandpa brushed himself off with one hand and tried to soothe Barney with the other. "Emily and Barney were protecting you, my dear, that's what. They thought I was a burglar, and they were ready to do battle." He pointed at the knife and the spray can on the floor.

Marjorie gave a little gasp. "Emily, you're incredible! You are the bravest girl I've ever known. Really, I—"

Emily couldn't bear it. She pulled herself away from their comforting arms and backed across the kitchen. "No, I'm not," she said shakily. "I'm not any of those things. I'm a dirty rat and you might as well know it."

And right then, with Grandpa, Marjorie, and Barney staring at her and the smell of hairspray heavy in the air, she told them exactly what she had done the night before.

13 · The End of the Project

"I just can't believe it," Emily's mother said. "I can't believe you would deliberately frighten another human being almost out of her wits. And then the next night try to drive off a burglar with a can of hairspray. What if it hadn't been Grandpa? Think of that!" Her mother stared across the kitchen table at Emily as if she had never seen her before. They had been sitting there for a half hour, ever since Emily had retreated from the grim silence of Grandpa's house, slipping out before Grandpa and Marjorie came downstairs. She had lain awake for hours remembering Grandpa's stunned expression and Marjorie's hurt silence as she told her story.

"I don't understand how your grandfather happened to come home during the night, anyway," her mother said. "He was supposed to be away for two nights."

Emily licked her dry lips. "The meeting ended earlier than he expected. He called Marjorie last night while I was taking a shower and said he was on his way home. She came in to tell me before she went to bed, but I pretended to be asleep."

Might as well confess it all. Let her mother know what kind of daughter she was raising. Maybe she would be lucky and Tony and the twins would turn out better.

"What's going on here?" It was her father, still in his pajamas and robe but with a wary look in his eye.

"Your father came home from his meeting at four o'clock this morning," Emily's mother told him. "Marjorie knew he was coming, but Emily didn't. She thought he was a burglar, and she attacked him with hairspray and a butcher knife. And that isn't all. Night before last she—"

"—did something or other to make Marjorie believe there was a burglar around when there wasn't," her father finished. He poured himself a cup of coffee. "What was it, Emily?"

Emily glared at him. "You knew all the time. Why didn't you say so?"

"Because I knew you'd feel better if you admitted it yourself," he said. "Do you?"

"Do I what?"

"Feel better? I'm assuming that everyone knows now what a naughty girl you've been." Her father put his coffee cup on the table and sat down. "I recognized the beer cans the sheriff's men picked up on your grandfather's lawn. They were my brand—not a very popular one—and they were flattened the particular way I do it."

So that was how he knew.

"Grandpa and Marjorie hate me," Emily said. "Grandpa is pretending not to, and Marjorie doesn't say anything at all. But they hate me, and now you and Mom hate me, and Sally thinks what I did was awful. If Tony knew, he'd hate me, and if the twins were old enough they'd hate me, too. I might as well be dead."

As if responding to a cue, the twins started to cry in their room. Emily's mother stood up and then sat down again.

"Go ahead," Emily said dully. "They're probably hungry."

"They won't starve," her mother said. "Emily, you know we don't hate you. We certainly don't like the idea that you would try to terrify Marjorie and drive her away, but we don't hate you. We love you very much. And even if it was a foolhardy thing to do, I think you were very brave to try to stop Grandpa when you thought he was a real burglar breaking into the house."

Emily's father drained the last of his coffee and filled his cup again. "If you ask Emily, she'll probably say it took more nerve to tell her grandfather and Marjorie the truth than it did to attack the intruder. Right, Emily?"

Emily shrugged. She couldn't take much credit for having confessed; the words had just seemed to come out by themselves when Grandpa and Marjorie began praising her for her courage. And she was glad that she had said them. She felt lighter now, as if weights had slipped off her shoulders. It was surprising that her father understood that. Perhaps, Emily thought, he knew a lot of things but found it hard to tell her that he knew. Maybe she and her father were alike that way. It was a good feeling, and it was nice of her mother to let Polly and Jane cry for once, instead of dropping everything to take care of them. Emily guessed they did love her, in spite of the terrible way she had turned out.

"Did you tell Grandpa and Marjorie you were sorry?" her mother asked.

Emily nodded miserably.

"And what did they say?"

"Grandpa just patted my head. I don't think he knew what to say. And Marjorie didn't do anything." Emily's voice cracked as she relived those moments. "I guess I'd better go back," she said. "I think I ought to say I'm sorry once more."

Emily saw her parents exchange glances. "Daddy will go with you," her mother said. "I have to feed the babies."

"No." Emily and her father said it at the same time. "I have to go alone," Emily said, and her father added, "Yes, you do. Good girl, Emily."

Tony clattered downstairs as Emily went out the front door. "Where're you going?" he demanded. Emily heard her father call to him. "Come out in the kitchen, young man. You can't go outside till you've had your breakfast."

Emily trudged along the road, her head down, her eyes on the toes of the sneakers that had gotten her into so much trouble. *I won't cry,* she promised herself. *I'll just say I'm sorry once more, and then I'll leave them alone. Forever.*

"Good thing one of us is looking or we'd have had a head-on collision." Emily jumped, startled out of her thoughts, and stared at her grandfather. They were toe to toe. "You look as if you have a lot on your mind."

"I was coming to apologize to you and Marjorie."

"Because your mom and dad wanted you to?"

"No," Emily said. "It was my idea. Oh, Grandpa, I really am sorry."

He took her hand, and they turned off into the woods.

"I know you are," said Grandpa, pushing aside a prickly branch that reached across the trail. "And I was coming over to apologize to *you*. The trouble is, Emily, I didn't know what was going on in your head. Maybe you think I should have, but I didn't. I thought that when you heard I was married you'd be happy because I was happy." Emily winced. "It didn't occur to me that you'd think Marjorie was going to take your place. No one could, Emily. You're my first granddaughter. You're Emily, and you're absolutely special in my life."

Emily clutched his hand tighter, afraid that in spite of herself she was going to cry.

"We should have talked about my marriage as soon as I came home," he went on, "so you'd know how I felt and I'd know how you felt. You see, I love being a father and a grandfather, and I loved your Grandma Ellen with my whole heart." He stopped and lifted Emily's chin so that he could look right into her face. "Now I love Marjorie. I didn't think I was going to fall in love again, but it happened, and I'm very glad. I want you to be glad, too."

"I am," Emily said and was astonished to discover that she meant it. "I guess you really need the companionship."

Grandpa snorted and resumed walking. "People can call it companionship if they want to," he said. "Everyone seems kind of uncomfortable when older people say they're in love. But I'll tell you something, Emily, and you can believe it. What I feel for Marjorie is love. The kind that changes everything. If she decides she can't bear to live out here, we'll move into town—both of us. I know I said I intended to stay here always, but I won't let her be unhappy."

And I've made her want to leave, Emily thought. *I'm the one who did it.*

"Not that we've decided anything like that," Grandpa went on, exactly as if he were reading her mind. "This morning at breakfast Marjorie told me what happened to her at her uncle's cottage when she was a little girl. She should have told me before. Then I would have understood why she was so nervous. First thing next week I'm having an electronic alarm system installed, and I'm going to get another dog, too. She has a lot of faith in Barney, but I figure two dogs ought to make her feel twice as safe as one."

"I hope so," Emily said humbly.

"And if I have to go out of town again, you'll stay with her, won't you?"

Emily looked up at him. "Would she want me?"

"Why don't you ask her yourself?" Grandpa turned suddenly and led Emily off the path to where the woods met the back lawn of the house. The windows were open and Marjorie was playing the piano. The lovely rippling sound seemed like part of the June day.

"You're not going away again for a couple of weeks, are you?" Emily asked. "Sally invited me to go to a cottage with her family."

"I doubt if I'll have to leave again until sometime in August," Grandpa replied. "We'll all have a lot of time together before then."

The music stopped. "She's really a good piano player," Emily said.

Grandpa nodded. "Marjorie was wondering if you'd like her to give you some lessons," he said casually. "You could practice at our house. If you start as soon as you get back from your holiday, and you work hard, you could give the kids in your class quite a surprise in September."

A project, Emily thought. She was going to have a project after all.

"I'll think about it," she said. "I'll give it some very serious thought." Then Emily squeezed her grandfather's arm and laughed out loud, for no particular reason except that it was the very first time she had felt like laughing since summer vacation began.

About the Author

Betty Ren Wright has spent her life in Wisconsin. She grew up in Milwaukee, graduated magna cum laude from Milwaukee-Downer College, and worked for 30 years with a publishing company in Racine. She and her husband currently live in Kenosha, Wisconsin.

Her literary career includes over 35 picture books, and her short stories have appeared in such publications as the *Alfred Hitchcock Mystery Magazine* and the *Saturday Evening Post*. This is her first novel.